VICIOUS VOLLEYBALL

Slamming the ball with an open palm, Chris sent it whizzing over the net, straight at Joe. Before he could bring up his hands to catch the ball, it caught him—hard, in the stomach.

"Are you all right?" Chris called. She and her partner, Tammy, were practicing serves. Frank and Joe were supposed to retrieve the balls and return them to the girls.

"Sure, fine," Joe insisted, refusing to rub his sore belly. He decided to stand clear and chase the balls instead of trying to catch them.

One of Tammy's serves bounced so hard off the sand that it rolled over to Joe's end of the court. Joe grabbed the runaway ball and trotted back with it, watching as Chris launched herself, preparing to serve again.

It was such a beautiful preparation that Joe felt like applauding. But before he could, Chris's hand struck the ball.

Instead of the expected *thwack* of hand against leather there was a sudden, blinding flash and a deafening explosion!

Books in THE HARDY BOYS CASEFILES® Series

Available from ARCHWAY Paperbacks

SPIKED!

FRANKLIN W. DIXON

AN ARCHWAY PAPERBACK
Published by POCKET BOOKS

New York   London   Toronto   Sydney   Tokyo   Singapore

AN ARCHWAY PAPERBACK *Original*

An Archway Paperback published by
POCKET BOOKS, a division of Simon & Schuster Inc.
1230 Avenue of the Americas, New York, NY 10020

Copyright © 1991 by Simon & Schuster Inc.
Produced by Mega-Books of New York, Inc.

ISBN: 0-671-73094-0

First Archway Paperback printing December 1991

10 9 8 7 6 5 4 3 2 1

THE HARDY BOYS, AN ARCHWAY PAPERBACK and colophon are registered trademarks of Simon & Schuster Inc.

THE HARDY BOYS CASEFILES is a trademark of Simon & Schuster Inc.

Cover art by Brian Kotzky

Printed in the U.S.A.

IL 6+

SPIKED!

Chapter

1

"GAME, LENZ AND OSTEEN." The voice over the loudspeakers drowned out the sound of crashing breakers at the beach volleyball court on southern California's Laguna Beach. "Match score: one, Lenz and Osteen; zero, Conlin and Donahue."

The crowd of approximately a thousand, which filled the bleachers on both sides of the court, erupted in raucous cheers. Joe Hardy, sitting in the center of the third row next to his brother, Frank, absently wiped the sweat trickling from his blond hair.

"What is it, a hundred and ten degrees out here?" he demanded.

"I told you to change clothes before we came to the games," Frank reminded him, sipping a jumbo-size Hi-Kick soda. Frank, who at eighteen was a year older than his brother, looked cool in colorful surfer's shorts, tank top, and sunglasses, with a bicycle cap covering his dark hair. He glanced at Joe, who was so pink he looked like uncooked steak in a polo shirt and long khaki pants.

"We were late," Joe protested. "It took me half an hour to sweet-talk two press passes from the hotel desk clerk. By the time she gave in, the tournament had already started. No way was I going to miss more of it to unpack!"

He grabbed Frank's soda and took a long sip. "Ugh," he said. "Too sweet."

"It's all they're selling at the refreshment stand," Frank said wryly. "Could that be because the tournament's sponsored by the Frosty Company, manufacturers of Hi-Kick soda?"

"They'll never make money with a taste like this." Joe handed the cup back.

The brothers turned back to await the start of the second game of the tournament's first set. Ever since the previous summer, when Joe had been introduced to the sport in Florida, he'd become a fanatic about beach volleyball. The regular game of six to a side he could take or leave, but beach volleyball with two to a side was fast and exciting—everything that appealed to him. When Frank and Joe had arrived at the South Coast Surf Club that morning, Joe had immediately spotted the poster announcing the First Annual Hi-Kick Beach Volleyball Tournament.

"Now I can show you how the game's really

played!'' he'd said enthusiastically as he read off the list of players from a bulletin board in the hotel lobby. "Wow, I've heard of these guys! Scooter Lenz and Peter Osteen from La Jolla. They're one of the top teams. Look, they're playing the U.S. champions this morning—Brad Conlin and Mark Donahue.'' Still reading, Joe had whistled softly. "Frosty's put a hundred thousand dollars in prize money into this competition. Fifty thousand each to the winning men's and women's teams!''

"Very interesting,'' Frank had said with a yawn as he picked up his suitcase to go to their room. The brothers' parents had sprung this summer getaway on them as a surprise just a couple of days before, and Frank hadn't had a good night's sleep the past two nights because of packing for the trip and the overnight flight to California. "I'm going upstairs to take a shower. Then I'm going to hit the beach.''

Well, they *were* on the beach, Frank reminded himself—bunched in with 998 other fans to watch four guys punch a volleyball back and forth over a net. The sun was so blindingly bright that Frank could hardly see the game even with sunglasses on. But in the distance, beyond the court, he could make out surfers gliding atop the Pacific breakers and closer in beautiful girls and body-builder guys sauntering along the crescent-shaped southern California beach. He was really tempted to make a break for it and join them. The Hardys hadn't been to California

3

in a while, and Frank wanted to enjoy the beaches.

The sound of the referee's whistle interrupted Frank's thoughts as game two of the match began. While the referee climbed a ladder at one side of center court, Frank watched Mark Donahue cradle the ball in his right hand. Joe had told him that at six feet two inches Donahue was the shortest male player in the entire competition. The muscles that bulged on his arms and legs as he took a step away from the back line made it obvious why he was among the top beach volley-ball contenders in the world.

His partner, Brad Conlin, had the leaner build and long blond hair of a surfer. His muscles were tensed like those of a weight lifter as Mark prepared to serve.

As Frank watched, Donahue charged forward, threw the ball high, then leapt about three feet off the sand to slam the ball with an overhead smash.

As the ball hummed over the net faster than a cruise missile, Frank decided there was no way for Lenz or Osteen to return the serve. Even as he was telling himself this, Frank saw Peter Osteen fling himself toward the ball to land full length on the sand. He got one hand under the ball and bumped it up to his partner. As Scooter Lenz tapped the ball straight up, Osteen sprang to his feet and slammed the ball down into the sand halfway between the opposing team.

"That was incredible!" Frank leapt to his feet as the crowd went wild. "Did you see the way he smashed that ball?"

"What'd I tell you?" Joe said over the noise of the loudspeakers. "These guys are amazing athletes! It takes muscle to make those moves on loose sand, and skill to maneuver with only one guy to back you up."

"Like a combination of pro tennis and regular volleyball," Frank agreed, impressed in spite of himself.

Frank watched Lenz and Osteen giving each other a high five. Osteen, with his curly red hair and six-foot-six, heavily muscled build, looked like a Viking in surfing baggies, blue tank top, and white Hi-Kick cap with the bill folded up. Lenz was much darker but just as large, with black curls escaping from under his Hi-Kick cap and a determined set to his strong jaw. Frank could see from the way they treated each other that the partners were good friends as well as teammates.

"These are permanent teams, right?" he asked his brother as the audience settled down and the next play began.

"Sure," Joe answered. "Men and women, both. There're major bucks in this sport, Frank. I read that Conlin and Donahue made about seventy-five thousand dollars each last year, *plus* endorsements and stuff."

Frank nodded. "The Frosty Company's sure getting its advertising value out of sponsoring

5

this contest." His eyes took in one of the six-foot-tall inflated mock-ups of Hi-Kick soft drink bottles that adorned each corner of the court and the table near the court covered with coolers and paper cups filled with Hi-Kick. Even the teenage ball-catchers who hovered behind each team wore Hi-Kick caps and T-shirts. There was no way the crews of TV news teams could avoid filming the Hi-Kick logo.

"Yeah, they'd better," replied Joe, fanning himself with a brochure, "if they expect to cut into SuperJuice's business. SuperJuice has always been number one in the sports drink market."

"Hey, wait," Frank said, interrupting as he peered at the huge scoreboard, also decorated with the blue-and-gold Hi-Kick logo. "The score-board says this game's tied at zero. I thought Osteen won the point."

"You have to be serving to get a point," Joe corrected. "Otherwise, it's just a 'side out.' The next serve switches to your side."

Frank nodded and turned back to watch Scooter Lenz serve. He stood just behind the back line and hit the ball underhand so that it soared over thirty feet in the air before coming down in the other court.

"All right, Scooter!" a fan yelled right in Frank's ear. "Dynamite high-ball!"

Trying to ignore the ringing in his ear, Frank watched as Conlin positioned himself under the serve and popped the ball to his partner, moving close to the net to await the setup. As Donahue hit it up in perfect position for a spike like the one Osteen had just made, Conlin jumped high. Across the net, Osteen leapt up, too, expecting the spike. But at the last second, Conlin only tapped the ball, causing it to arc over Osteen's outstretched arms and drop dead in the sand. Side out, Frank told himself, letting his breath out.

"Way to go, Marco! Fantastic dink!" called out a fan, making Frank's other ear buzz.

"Still zero–zero," Frank commented. "It could be a long time between points at this rate. A game's what, fifteen?"

"Fifteen points," Joe agreed. "And you have to win by at least two points."

"They're going to be totally wiped out," Frank said. "In this heat, playing that hard—"

"Whoever wants it most will win," Joe finished for him, wiping sweat from his face as he followed the action.

"Well, you were right about one thing. They earn their money."

As the match continued, Frank found himself captivated by the impressive jump serves, towering high-ball serves, perfectly timed blocks, and soft dink shots hit just out of reach. Because there were so many more side outs than points, the sun had climbed to the top of the sky and started to descend before the score evened up at two games to two.

"Next team to win a game wins the match." Joe sat up taller in his seat as the exhausted players took a break in the shade of a Hi-Kick awning. "Osteen looks bad."

Frank peered at Osteen, who was resting on one knee under the awning and breathing heavily. His face was flushed and sweaty, and when he stood up, his legs looked a little shaky. Scooter Lenz, his teammate, muttered something to him. Osteen shook his head, then walked back out to start the next game.

"You're right," Frank said. "Looks like he has sunstroke or something."

He wondered privately whether the game would be called, but the referee didn't seem to notice Osteen's condition. He climbed the ladder to the top of the net and blew his whistle so play could begin.

"Way to go, Osteen!" Joe yelled. At least the rest of the crowd had quieted down somewhat, Frank thought thankfully. The heat seemed to have affected them as well.

"Set point!" announced the loudspeakers nearly an hour later. Frank snapped out of his heat-induced doldrums to see a score of 14–15, Conlin-Donahue, on the board. He looked at the court. All four players appeared ragged and were dripping with sweat, but Osteen was by far the worst off. Swaying a little on his feet, he signaled a pause and then trudged through the sand to the Hi-Kick table. As he grabbed a blue paper cup and gulped down the soda, the crowd supporting the current champions rumbled impatiently.

"Play ball," the referee called finally, and Osteen, looking a little revived, trudged back to the court.

When play resumed, Brad Conlin was serving. Osteen hit the serve first and passed the ball to Scooter Lenz in the middle of the court. Lenz bent at the knees, clasped his hands low, and tapped the ball straight up in a perfect set. Osteen leapt to spike the ball down at an angle that couldn't be returned.

His jump wasn't high enough, though. Frank yelled as Conlin, who was ready and waiting, smashed Osteen's shot back over the net.

Lenz saw the ball coming and made a desperate lunge to retrieve it. It landed inches from him, just inside the boundary of the court.

"Match to Conlin and Donahue!" Joe cried as the crowd cheered and rose in a standing ovation for all four players.

Frank watched the exhausted players—two triumphant and two destroyed—move toward the net to shake hands with their opponents. Scooter Lenz's head was hanging low on his chest. He was the perfect picture of defeat, Frank thought.

"Boy, what a game!" Joe said, forgetting all about the heat in his enthusiasm. "Did you see how Conlin—"

"Joe, look!" Frank interrupted, standing up and pointing at the court. As Joe followed his gaze, the older Hardy stared at Peter Osteen.

The redheaded player had crumpled to the sand and was lying there, his body twitching and his legs thrashing uncontrollably. His fellow players had turned toward him in shock.

"Osteen's down!" a fan screamed and suddenly there was a rush of spectators from the bleachers.

"Come on!" Frank shouted, moving down to the front of the bleachers. He pushed toward the edge of the court, where a group of players, coaches, and Hi-Kick officials huddled over the downed player. Several television crews had crowded around, too, their camera lenses aimed at Osteen. They backed off only after one of the officials agreed to give them an interview.

"Give him air!" A pair of medics with Hi-Kick patches on their white jackets ran toward Osteen. The fans moved closer, anyway, their curiosity overpowering their caution.

Frank and Joe broke through to the front ranks of the crowd. From where he was standing Frank could see that Osteen's face had turned a dangerous shade of green. As the medics bent over him, the spasms in the player's limbs were growing weaker. Staring at the stricken teen, Frank only heard Joe's voice.

"Frank," Joe was whispering, staring at the player in shock. "It looks like he's stopped breathing!"

Chapter

2

"COME ON, OSTEEN. Breathe!" Joe clenched his fists, frustrated at not being able to help. Both Frank and Joe were experts at CPR, but Joe knew the tournament officials would never let a couple of teenagers near a player in trouble.

"The ambulance," someone in the crowd announced as the noise of a siren approached. The hundreds of fans who'd surrounded the court turned to watch as a team of paramedics leapt out of their ambulance and raced with a stretcher to the scene.

"Ladies and gentlemen," announced a voice on the loudspeakers, "we have a medical emergency. Repeat, a medical emergency. The remainder of today's tournament will be delayed until further notice. Those who desire ticket refunds should go to the tournament office at the Surf Club. Please avoid the court area as you leave."

"Okay, move back," Joe ordered the crowd, turning to push the fans gently backward. "Give the medics room to move."

Frank came to his aid. Several fans grumbled angrily, but gradually they either wandered away or returned to their seats to await word on Osteen's condition.

Then Joe heard more sirens and peered down the road. "Police," he said to Frank.

Joe stepped back as one of the tournament officials, a short, middle-aged man in white pants and a blue knit shirt with the Hi-Kick logo made his way to the stretcher. He seemed very tense and kept wiping his forehead with a soggy handkerchief. As soon as he heard the wailing of the sirens, the man froze midstep and frowned. "Who called the cops?" he demanded.

"Uh, I did, sir." It was Osteen's partner, Scooter Lenz. Joe had noticed him following anxiously beside the official and had felt sorry for him. "We need the cops, right?"

"What for?" the little man shouted hoarsely, applying his handkerchief to his face again. "Because Peter keeled over from too much sun? That's illegal now?"

"Sir?" Joe Hardy stepped forward hesitantly, glancing down at Peter Osteen's inert body as the paramedics carried it past him. What he saw made his heart skip a beat. Peter's mouth hung open, his eyes were closed, and his body lay still. "Uh, is Peter still alive?"

"Alive? Alive!" The question seemed to send

the official into a fit of rage. "Of course he's alive. Dead people don't play beach volleyball tournaments, young man."

"I was just wondering. Because if he had died, the police would have to ask questions and decide on the cause of death."

"Questions?" The nervous man glanced toward the ambulance, where the paramedics were just slamming the back doors shut.

"It's standard procedure," said Frank, backing up his brother. "Besides, you'll need help handling this crowd."

"Who *are* you guys?" the official demanded as the ambulance pulled away and two police cruisers pulled into its place. "You act like cops."

"Our dad was a cop," Joe explained quickly. "And we've done a lot of detective work ourselves. You might have read about us in the papers a while back when we solved a case for a movie studio in L.A. I'm Joe Hardy, and this is my brother, Frank."

The man's eyes bugged out, and his handkerchief hung forgotten from his fist. "*You're* the Hardy brothers?" Then slowly his eyes lit up. He looked like a condemned prisoner who'd just figured out how to escape, Joe thought.

"This could be a stroke of luck," the man said, lowering his voice. "I'm Richard Prindle, head of promotion for the Frosty Company. This tournament was my idea, and I have to make sure it generates great publicity for Hi-Kick or I'm in big trouble. Maybe we could—''

The sirens cut off abruptly. Three men in uniform and two in civilian clothes were climbing out of the cars. "Just what I need," Prindle moaned. "A sick volleyball champ *and* a scandal for the newspapers. Excuse me, boys. Might as well get this over with."

Prindle marched over to meet the officers. The other officials and players watched him go. Everyone was very upset, and one of the female players had begun crying.

"It wasn't the sun that did it," a voice said in Joe's ear.

Startled, Joe turned to find Scooter Lenz standing next to him. "It wasn't?" he said, taken off guard at having one of his favorite athletes speak to him. "What did do it, then?"

"Too much sugar." Scooter's eyes flicked from Joe to Frank. "Or too little. Osteen was a diabetic. Prindle didn't tell you 'cause he thinks any weakness in the players weakens the show."

"You're saying he had a diabetic reaction?" Frank said, taking a step closer. "Did you tell the paramedics? If they know, they may be able to save him."

"Sure I told them," Scooter said, offended. "What do you think, I'd let him die to keep Prindle happy?"

"Sorry," Frank said, embarrassed. "It's just— well, we flew in from the East Coast this morning and I guess we're pretty beat."

"Yeah, but you're detectives, right? I heard you talking to Prindle. Are you going to hang around for a while?"

"Yeah," said Joe. "We're staying at the Surf Club. Why?"

"Well," he said, kicking at the sand with one huge foot, "I'm sure what my partner had was one of those seizures, all right, but what I wonder is, how come? I mean, a diabetic's blood sugar level has to get either real high or real low to set off a reaction like that, and Osteen double-checks his blood sugar so many times during a tourney, it couldn't possibly have gotten out of hand."

"Then what do you think caused the attack?"

Scooter shrugged. "I don't know enough about it, I guess. But I do have a funny feeling about this, and I figure it can't hurt to know how to reach you guys."

While Frank gave Scooter their room number at the Surf Club, Joe noticed one of the plain-clothes detectives, a burly redhead, approaching them across the sand.

"Scooter Lenz?" the man asked. He flashed a leather case with a gold badge inside. "Detective Sergeant Dan O'Boyle, Laguna Beach P.D. Could I have a word with you, please?"

"Sure," the volleyball champion said uneasily. "Uh, how is he?"

The detective closed his eyes and sucked in a lungful of hot air. "He died on the way to the hospital, I'm afraid. He went into a brief coma, then slipped away. I'm sorry." He hesitated, then said more gently, "Mr. Prindle tells me you were the last person to see him alone."

At the news that his partner was dead, Scooter had become deathly pale. Now he stammered as he tried to answer the detective without crying.

Joe felt as though he'd been hit with a sledgehammer. He'd been following Peter Osteen's career for months. He couldn't believe that the nineteen-year-old champ could actually die moments after playing so well.

"Excuse us," Frank said to the detective and Scooter, pulling Joe away. "I think Mr. Prindle wants to talk to us."

"I can't get over it," Joe kept saying as his older brother steered him over the firm, hard sand. "He looked great out there one instant. Then the next—"

"Here's what we're going to do," Frank said in a low breath, tightening his grip on his brother's arm. "We're going to find Prindle and offer to look into the situation for him. We'll convince Prindle that finding out what really happened to Osteen is better for the Frosty Company than everybody thinking it was careless about a player's health."

"What do you mean, 'what really happened to Osteen'?" Joe asked. "You think Scooter's right about something being fishy?"

"I think more than that," Frank said grimly. "Remember that volunteer stint I did at Bayport Hospital? We had diabetics come into the emergency room. People with hyperglycemic reactions don't usually jerk and twitch like Osteen did. They just slow down, like they're falling asleep, and quietly slip into a coma. People who twitch around a lot, *then* fall unconscious, are more likely to have been poisoned."

Joe stared at him. "How sure are you about this?" he demanded.

"It's only a hunch," Frank admitted, "but I definitely smell a rat. Besides," he added dryly, "we're here for two weeks, right? Two whole weeks with nothing to do."

"Yeah," Joe said as they continued their search for Prindle. "Nothing but surfing, swimming, lying around on the beach, talking to pretty girls—"

The loudspeakers announced just then that the tournament would close for the day—without mentioning Peter's death. Hundreds of grumbling fans began moving toward the parking lot as Joe and Frank found Prindle standing near the cruisers. They presented him with their offer. Prindle, looking haggard, merely nodded his head meekly.

"Meet me at the Surf Club in twenty minutes," he finally said. "Our tournament offices are in two large Winnebago trailers in the parking lot. The one closer to the clubhouse is mine."

"We'll be there," Frank agreed.

As Prindle hurried away, Joe asked his brother, "What now?"

"Let's find the other team—Brad Conlin and

17

Mark Donahue,'' Frank said, leading the way back toward the court. "If we're looking for suspects, those two would have had a lot to lose, right?"

"Yeah, but they're all volleyball players, Frank," Joe protested. "You don't think—" He paused midsentence, noticing that Detective O'Boyle was now interviewing the Hi-Kick film crew. He wanted to listen in on their conversation and said so to Frank. Joe filled his brother in when he returned. "He asked them if they'd noticed anything suspicious this morning. But the guy who spoke for them said no. He said something about just minding their business and getting the job done."

"Great," Frank said. "With friends like that, Osteen didn't need enemies. Look, there are Conlin and Donahue."

Joe followed Frank toward the two players, who were talking at the far end of the net with their backs to the Hardys.

Motioning to Joe to be quiet, Frank moved closer toward the two. But even Joe could hear Donahue when he erupted loudly, "A lot of nerve, asking those questions! Like we're criminals! I should have—"

"Take it easy," Joe heard Conlin answer. "Just keep cool, and don't blow it. You don't want to—"

Joe wasn't able to hear any more. Afraid the players would notice them, Frank had backed off and signaled to Joe to move off with him.

"Those two aren't in the mood for questions," Frank muttered to Joe. "It's time to go see Prindle anyway."

They walked the short distance down the beach to the Surf Club complex. Joe took in the beautiful curved beach with sunbathers settled in on blankets and a group of hotel guests tucked under identical yellow beach umbrellas. A boy and a girl were flying a kite while a German shepherd that had escaped from somewhere frolicked illegally in the waves. It looked exactly the way Joe had pictured it when his father had first told them about their trip. Now that they were here, though, all Joe could think about was a volleyball player's death and how he and Frank might have to solve another mystery. Joe sighed. He guessed the detecting urge was in the Hardy blood.

"Wow. Air conditioning!" Joe said as he and Frank entered Mr. Prindle's comfortable trailer office. "Does that feel good."

"Sit down, sit down." Prindle, still obviously distraught, was gesturing to two chairs facing his desk. "Make yourselves at home. Can I get you something to drink?"

Joe sat in the chair nearer the desk, noting the piles of manila folders, glossy photographs, and printed literature that cluttered every inch of available space. "Thanks," he said to Prindle. "What do you have?"

Prindle opened the door of a small refrigerator beside his desk and peered inside. "Frosty Cola,

Frosty Orange, Frosty Lemon—and plenty of Hi-Kick.''

Joe exchanged a glance with his brother. "Two orange sodas would be fine," he said.

As Prindle pulled out two cans, popped the tops, and handed them to the brothers, Joe noticed that the executive's hands were shaking.

"I'm very worried," Prindle blurted out abruptly as he sat back down at his desk. "There's been some funny business going on around here. Now that Peter is dead—" He hesitated, then said, "Sorry, I can't really believe it. But if you two think there might be something—irregular—about his death, the rest of what's happened might turn out to be more important than I'd thought. Or maybe there's no connection, after all. I hope not, but—"

Frank raised a hand in the air to stop Prindle's nervous chatter. "Just start from the top, sir."

"Sorry." Prindle cleared his throat. "First of all, this Hi-Kick assignment is my big break at the Frosty Company. We're trying to carve out a place for ourselves in the sports drink market, and using pro beach volleyball was my idea. This is a sport with a future. It gets lots of TV time already, and the players are becoming known. But they are still a lot cheaper to sign for endorsements than pro football players. So you get value for your money."

Joe sipped his soda and nodded. Prindle was talking very fast. Either he was in shock, Joe decided, or he was trying to hide something. Or maybe both.

"It's been a lot of work so far," the promotion man continued. "Arranging to get the top players in the game and hiring a good filmmaker. A lot of work. But finally everything was coming together," Prindle went on. "And then we started getting letters."

"What letters?" asked Frank.

Prindle unlocked the middle drawer of his desk and pulled out a manila folder. "Someone's been trying to scare us out of holding the tournament," he explained. "We started getting threatening notes at our office headquarters." He opened the folder to let the brothers see. "Then a couple of players received anonymous phone calls telling them to drop out of the competition."

"Which players?" Joe asked, watching Frank page through the notes. The messages were made up of individual letters in all sizes and styles cut from magazines.

"Conlin and Donahue for certain. Maybe others who haven't told me. And now a player is dead. I knew Peter had diabetes, but I never knew a guy so careful about his physical health."

Joe read the letter Frank was looking at out loud. " 'The Frosty Company sells junk to its customers! The time has come to pay for your crimes! Stop the Hi-Kick tournament or else!' Sounds like a pretty extreme reaction to a soft drink," he joked to Prindle.

Prindle wasn't laughing. He had become silent and his gaze was fixed. "What's that?" he finally asked out loud, continuing to stare at the same spot.

The boys turned and saw a sheet of paper lying on the floor near the door. Joe stood up and moved over to pick up the paper. He wasn't surprised to see another message written from letters cut out of magazines.

Joe laid it on Prindle's desk.

Prindle read the short note silently, and a moan escaped his throat. "This one's really insane," he said, handing it to Frank.

" 'Frosty can be dangerous to people's health!' " Frank read out loud. " 'Stop the games, or you'll regret it!' "

Chapter
3

SO THERE REALLY IS something going on here!
Frank thought grimly.

Prindle rested his forearms on his desk and
leaned over them. "Listen," he said, quietly taking in both boys. "The tournament is scheduled
to end here in four days, even with today's post-
ponement. After that, we take the winners on a
tour along the East and West coasts. I need to
know that no more disasters are going to happen. If someone is after my players, I want that
person stopped. Can I count on you to find out
whatever's going on here?"

Before Frank or Joe could answer, the door
swung open and a short, skinny man with
slicked-back dark hair popped his head inside.
"*Great* match, Prindle!" he said as Frank and
Joe turned to gaze at him. He wore a flower-

print shirt and bright red pants. "Shame about your player, Osteen, though. If there's anything I can do—"

"I don't need any help, Auerbach," Prindle growled. "And right now I'm busy."

"Don't let me interrupt," said the newcomer. "See you around."

"He sure seemed happy," Frank remarked after the man left. "Kind of inappropriate after the death of a player. Who *was* he?"

"Todd Auerbach," said Prindle angrily. "He's the public relations man for our biggest competitor, SuperJuice. They're based in Santa Ana, near here. He's been nosing around, offering endorsement contracts to some of the players. I saw him at the games this morning, so I'm not surprised that he stopped by to gloat. So—will you take this case?"

"You bet," said Joe. "We've already taken it, actually."

"Great." Prindle appeared to relax a little. "What can I do to help you?"

"You could use us as tournament workers," suggested Frank. "You know—say we're big volleyball fans and we've volunteered to help out. That way, maybe we can pick up information on the inside."

"No problem," said Prindle. "You can start tomorrow, first thing in the—"

Just then, the office door swung in again and an agitated-looking man strode in. Frank recognized the tall, thin man with the blond mustache as one of the Hi-Kick filmmakers who'd been talking to Detective O'Boyle earlier. He still wore his Hi-Kick T-shirt, but he'd switched his Hi-Kick cap for a regular baseball cap.

"Those cops confiscated every foot of film I shot today!" the man roared at Prindle before the executive could greet him. "They said it was *evidence!* I *need* that footage! I mean, I'm sorry Peter's dead, but it's not like they're going to find somebody taking a shot at him on my film."

"Hey, Ken, lighten up," said Prindle, smiling nervously. "I'm sure you'll get the film back and in good condition. We have to cooperate with the law, right?"

The blond man hesitated, then calmed down a little. "I guess so," he admitted. "But if they ruin one frame of that film—"

"Ken Chaplin, I want to you meet Frank and Joe Hardy," Prindle interrupted. "They love beach volleyball and have volunteered to work at the tournament. Can you use some help?"

Frank smiled to look friendly as Ken sized them up, his gripe already forgotten.

"Actually, I could use a couple of guys tomorrow. We're scheduled to shoot Chris Welles demonstrating the jump serve."

"Just tell us where to go, and we'll be there," said Joe.

"All right," said Chaplin with a nod. "Tomorrow morning, nine o'clock. Just ask for Chris Welles, and someone will show you where to go. See you then."

He started out the door, saying to Prindle, "Just do me a favor, okay? Could you push the cops to give back my film right away?"

That evening, after an early seafood dinner at the huge outdoor dining area on the beach, Frank and Joe relaxed on the terrace of their second-story hotel room. Right then, the boys were enjoying a perfect sunset while their feet were propped up on the railing.

But their minds weren't on the scenery.

"Maybe someone's trying to get some money out of the company," Joe suggested, shifting in his plastic chair. "Someone figures Frosty is a big, rich conglomerate with a reputation to protect. It might pay plenty to avoid trouble."

"But the notes haven't mentioned money. Not yet, anyway." Frank frowned, gazing out into the distance. "We'll have to find out if Osteen had any enemies. It's possible the letters and his death aren't even connected."

"I don't know, Frank. I have a feeling they are. And if they are, we're dealing with some rough customers."

Frank nodded. He thought about all the people he'd met who were connected with the Frosty Company. He recalled Conlin telling Donahue to "Keep cool, and don't blow it," and wondered what that meant. He thought about that weird-looking Todd Auerbach and wondered if he was capable of murder. And why, he asked himself, was Richard Prindle so nervous all the time? Was he hiding something—something that the Hardys needed to know?

"I wish Dad were here," he said to Joe. "I'd like to know his thoughts on this."

"I'll tell you his thoughts," Joe said with a short laugh. "Summed up in two words: Be careful."

The next morning the Hardys had breakfast in their room so they could join the tournament workers early. From the lobby, they followed a winding corridor to the opposite end of the rambling hotel complex, where an entire wing that housed a gym, locker rooms, saunas, and spa had been rented for the volleyball players' use.

"Let's check this out," Frank said at the entrance to the men's locker room. He and Joe entered the low-ceilinged room to find a small group of players huddled together near the showers. They were talking in low tones and ignored Frank and Joe. They all had downcast expressions, Frank noticed and wondered if they were discussing Osteen.

"Frank. Over here." Joe was motioning to him from a row of lockers partway across the room. Frank joined him, reading the players' names on strips of masking tape stuck to each locker. Joe stood beside a locker with a tape that read 'Osteen.'

"It's unlocked," Joe whispered excitedly. He swung the door open and instantly saw that the locker had been cleared out.

27

"That must be his stuff." Frank nodded toward a stool near the locker. A pile of items was stacked on top of it. "They must be getting ready to ship it back to his family."

"How do you know it's Osteen's?"

"Look what's on top." Frank picked up a small black box with an LCD display window at the top and the word *Glucograph* in white block letters across the bottom. He turned it over to inspect the buttons and slot at one end and the hinged door in the bottom where batteries went. "I saw one of these once at the hospital. It's for monitoring blood sugar—"

"Can I help you guys?"

Frank stopped midsentence to stare up at the tallest volleyball player he'd seen so far. His incredible muscle tone was obvious even under his shirt, and the frown on his face was very threatening.

"Yes, you can," Joe said easily. "I'm Joe Hardy. This is my brother, Frank. We've just been hired on as general assistants for the tournament, and we're supposed to find Chris Welles. Do you know where he is?"

A flicker of amusement appeared on the player's face. "I'm not sure." He gazed over Joe's shoulder and called out, "Hey, George! This guy wants to know where Chris is."

Two powerful hands clamped down on Joe's shoulders and spun him around. Joe found himself staring up at a handsome, scowling face framed by curly, blond hair.

Frank figured the stranger was at least five inches taller than Joe, and even more muscular than the first guy.

"What do you want with Chris Welles?" the blond giant demanded.

The big hands remained clenched on Joe's shoulders. Frank stepped forward protectively. "Take it easy," he said to the athlete, and Joe pulled back a step to get loose.

The volleyball player named George didn't want to take it easy, though. He stepped forward, grabbed a handful of Frank's shirt, and pushed him back. Frank didn't have a chance to brace himself and was propelled straight through a swinging door that led to an outdoor lounge area. Before Joe could react, the giant had grabbed his shirt, too, and Joe was sailing through the swinging door after his brother.

As Frank and Joe struggled to regain their balance, the blond athlete strode out after them. Shaking a fist under Joe's nose, he growled, "Mess around with Chris and I'll bust your face for you! Understand?"

Chapter

JOE *DIDN'T* UNDERSTAND, and it was clear from Frank's expression that he didn't either. Who *was* this guy, and why was he pulling this cave-man routine? Joe swatted the hand away from his face and glared at his attacker.

"What's your problem?" he protested. "I was just—"

George bored in, sticking an index finger in Joe's chest. "I don't have a problem. *You* have a problem."

Joe felt the anger building inside. A voice in the back of his mind told him to be cool, but this dude was primed to fight, and Joe wasn't going to be pushed around any more.

"Listen, whoever you are, get out of my face! I won't tell you again!"

The stranger's scowl gave way to an ugly grin. "Okay. That's it. You asked for it."

As Joe braced himself for the guy's first move, a girl's voice shouted behind them. *"George!"* she cried, sounding very angry.

The volleyball player flinched, then backed away in confusion and embarrassment.

"What do you think you're doing?" demanded the voice.

Over the athlete's shoulder, Joe spotted a beautiful, blond girl. When she approached him, Joe saw that she was as tall as he was. He looked directly into her deep blue eyes. She glanced at Joe long enough to make him realize his mouth was hanging open. Then she turned to glare at George again. "Uh, h-hi," George stammered, staring down at his feet. "I was just—I mean—this guy here—" He stopped, not knowing what to say.

The girl's eyes shifted impatiently to Joe. "Are you okay?" she asked matter-of-factly. "I'm Chris Welles, this lunk's unofficial nursemaid."

Joe returned the smile. Then he realized what she'd said.

"Chris. You're Chris? Oh! Uh, I'm—Joe. Joe Hardy. This is my brother, Frank. We were supposed to find you this morning—that is, until this guy tried to stop us. We're assisting with the film shoot."

"Ah. My chance at the big screen," Chris joked, reaching out to shake Joe's hand. She smiled brightly at him, ignoring George's low growl. Joe glanced nervously at George, noting that his face had turned a bright, angry red.

"Don't worry, George, I'll introduce you," Chris said, and laughed. She released Joe's hand, saying, "The big clown with no manners is George Ritt. Go on, George, say hello, and try to smile."

George obviously didn't feel like smiling, but he forced his face into an almost pleasant expression and muttered something Joe couldn't decipher. Then he turned abruptly and reentered the men's locker room.

"Sorry about that," Chris said to Joe and Frank after he'd gone. "He has it in his head that I'm his property. I wish I knew where he got that idea. He has a habit of attacking any male who even mentions my name."

"Sounds like a nice guy," Frank said.

"You meet all types in this sport." Chris's expression suddenly brightened. "This film is going to be great. Wait till you see Tammy's serve. She's my partner. Let's go find her. The crew's probably setting up."

As the brothers followed her away from the clubhouse, Joe felt someone watching him. He glanced back to see that George had reappeared in the outdoor lounge area and was following their departure with a nasty expression on his face. Joe had the feeling there was going to be more trouble with the massive player sometime when Chris wasn't around.

Turning forward again, Joe saw that several volleyball courts had been set up on the beach behind the clubhouse. Ken Chaplin's helper was clearing the area of sunbathers and onlookers as Ken set up the equipment. Joe gave a low whistle, impressed with the quality of the cameras, lights, reflectors, and insulated film cases that lay in a pile on a plastic sheet.

A little to one side of the film crew, Joe saw a girl sitting on a beach chair, catching some sun. She spotted Chris and the Hardys coming and waved, smiling. As they walked across the court, she stood up—revealing that she was a couple of inches taller than Chris.

"This is my partner, Tammy Strauss," Chris said. "Tammy, meet Frank and Joe Hardy."

As Joe shook hands with Tammy, he marveled that two such good-looking and tall women could be partners. Tammy's light brown hair, cut very short, and her high cheekbones and friendly brown eyes, made her almost as attractive as Chris. He could tell from Frank's expression that he was thinking the same thing. Because of Frank's attachment to his girl, Callie Shaw, he barely noticed most other girls. These two were stunning, though. The fact that he had to look *up* to Tammy might have something to do with it, too, Joe thought slyly.

"Frank? Joe?" Chaplin, who was dressed in a Hi-Kick T-shirt and baseball cap as he had been the day before, motioned to them to join him. His helper—a muscular, older guy with wiry black hair going gray at the temples— looked up as the Hardys approached.

"I want to introduce you to my assistant

before we start," Chaplin said. "Vern Elliott's my right-hand man—assistant director, cameraman, lighting expert, editor—you name it. There's nothing in the film business he hasn't done. Vern, Frank and Joe Hardy. They'll be our gofers for today's shoot."

Vern winked, then went back to work. Joe thought he had seen a coldness in the older man's eyes, but it had all happened too quick to tell for sure. He did notice the tattoos on both of Vern's arms as he reached for a reflector, though. One depicted a dragon devouring a snake. The other one looked like a wild dog with a knife held between its teeth.

Ken continued briskly, "We'll be using two cameras. Vern will be stationary here, using the tripod. I'll use a hand-held camera, to get shots from different angles. I need you guys to retrieve the balls as the girls serve them."

He pointed to a huge bag next to the net that bulged with volleyballs. "Chris and Tammy will alternate, serving from opposite ends of the court, and you'll grab the balls and stuff them into these empty bags here, so we can keep filming without long breaks. We're on a tight schedule; they have a match this afternoon, and I promised their coach they wouldn't be out here too long. So stay on your toes. Understood?"

"No problem," Joe said, watching Chris warm up with a couple of stretching exercises.

"Isn't this net too low?" Frank asked Tammy.

"It's lower for women," she explained with a smile. "Seven and a half feet for us, eight and a half for men."

She was about to say more when Chaplin called, "Ready, girls? Crew? Frank, slate the cameras!"

Luckily, Frank had worked on small films before. He knew to pick up a set of clappers that was lying on the plastic sheet, hold it in front of Vern's camera and say, "*A* camera, mark!" Then he stuck the clappers in front of Chaplin's hand-held camera. "*B* camera, mark!" Then he ran back to his place opposite Tammy, ready to retrieve the balls.

"Okay, Chris," Chaplin shouted as he knelt and steadied the camera on his shoulder. "Let's see a monster serve, now."

Chris set herself five yards behind the end line and ran forward. Joe admired her coordination as she tossed the ball high and leapt up after it. Her body arched as her arm swung back, so that when the arm came forward all her strength was behind it.

Slamming the ball with an open palm, Chris sent it whizzing over the net, straight at Joe. Before he could bring up his hands to catch it, it caught *him*—hard, in the stomach.

"Are you all right?" called Chris. Joe looked up in time to catch a combination of concern and amusement on her face.

"Sure, fine," he insisted, refusing to rub his sore belly. "It surprised me, that's all." He stuffed the ball into the empty bag and decided to stand clear and just chase the balls wherever they rolled from then on. He wasn't crazy about being laughed at by beautiful girls.

Tammy's serve, Joe thought resentfully, wasn't quite so fast as Chris's, but since Tammy was so tall she was able to smash the ball at a steep angle. Joe watched as Frank ran helplessly after it and felt better.

The women alternated serves and Chaplin moved around them, sometimes kneeling, sometimes standing, and even lying on his back with the camera pointed straight up at the server.

When one of Tammy's serves bounced off the sand so hard that it rolled over to Joe's end of the court, Joe retrieved it for his brother.

Joe grabbed the runaway ball and trotted back with it, watching as Chris launched herself, preparing to strike the ball.

It was such a beautiful preparation that Joe felt like applauding. But before he could, Chris's hand struck the ball. To Joe's horror, instead of the expected *thwack* of hand against leather there was a sudden, blinding flash and a deafening explosion!

Chapter

5

"CHRIS!"

Joe dropped the volleyball and raced toward the player. Tammy made it to Chris just as Joe had snatched Chris's hand to see if it was okay. By the time Vern and Chaplin had joined them, it was obvious that no major harm had been done.

"I'm okay," Chris said shakily, staring at her hand as if it didn't belong to her. It had several minor burn marks on it, but they were already fading. "I can't believe it didn't hurt more than it did. It was so loud." She smiled sheepishly at the small crowd of onlookers that had gathered. "What happened? Did the ball just—explode?"

Frank had been picking up the shreds of exploded volleyball that lay on the court. Now he joined Joe, holding the rubber bits in his hand.

"The shreds are scorched," he said. "Maybe nitrous oxide."

The athletes and the film crew stared at him. "You mean it was a—a bomb?" Tammy demanded.

Joe picked out one piece of rubber, turned it over to inspect the back, and nodded. "A *kind* of bomb—the kind that's meant to scare and not hurt."

"What do you mean?" asked Chaplin.

"Someone planted a booby-trapped ball in the bag," Joe explained. "All they had to do was inflate a volleyball with an explosive gas like nitrous oxide. Then they'd paint the outside of the ball with an ammonium tri-iodide solution or something like it. That would act like a trigger, and the first time something smacked against it, it would set off an explosion. Unfortunately, that something was Chris's hand."

"The explosion is really pretty minor," Frank added. "So there was no real danger of anyone getting hurt."

"You and your brother certainly know an awful lot about bombs," Chaplin said, eyeing Frank suspiciously.

Frank shrugged modestly. "We've read detective novels since we were little kids. You learn a lot that way."

"But who would do something like this?" Chris asked.

Tammy frowned. "Maybe it has something to do with that phone call."

"What call?" Joe glanced at Frank.

"We thought it was just a dumb joke," said Chris. "Tammy has a house here, and I'm staying with her during the tournament. A few nights ago some weirdo called and started saying we'd better quit the tournament or we'd be sorry."

"Was it a man or a woman?" Frank asked.

"I couldn't be sure," replied Tammy. "The voice was obviously disguised."

"Great," said Chaplin, disgusted. "So now the maniac's trying to sabotage us."

Joe eyed him curiously. "What do you mean?"

"You haven't heard?" Chaplin answered. "A bunch of players have gotten phone calls like Tammy's. Some of my equipment was damaged—one of my telephoto lenses was scratched up, and I had to send my best tape deck to the shop."

"Where did all this happen?" Frank asked.

"In our trailer, next to Prindle's. Someone picked the lock a couple of nights back. I've put in a security system since then, because people keep—"

He was interrupted by a gasp from Chris.

"Could Peter Osteen's death have any connection with this?"

"Whoa." Joe put a hand on Chris's shoulder. "As far as we know now, Osteen probably died of hypoglycemic shock. And as for this stuff, who can tell? It could be just coincidence. A practical joker who happens to like beach volleyball."

Chaplin smiled thinly. "Fat chance that they're

39

not connected. Believe me, brother, if I didn't need the money, I wouldn't stick around."

Chris turned away abruptly.

"Are you okay?" Joe asked, moving over to her.

She nodded, swallowing hard. "Sorry. I was thinking about Peter Osteen. We dated last year." She smiled furtively. "He sent Nadia into incredible fits."

"Nadia?" echoed Joe.

"Nadia Galinova, our coach. She believes that mixing dating and sports is lethal. She told Peter to stay away from me, and he told her to mind her own business. She said he didn't care about my career, which was silly. But they got at each other so much that I finally stopped seeing Peter."

"You play a lot." Frank tactfully changed the subject.

"Three months is all this year," she answered, forcing a smile. "I start college this fall, so I won't play professionally again until next summer. This is the big event of the year for us. Unless they cancel it because of what's been happening." Chris was obviously unhappy at the thought.

"I doubt that they will," said Tammy. "They've put an awful lot of money into this event. I can't imagine the Frosty Company throwing away all of that unless we get some really ghastly publicity or some solid proof that something's wrong."

40

"Speaking of publicity," said Chaplin, "it's almost eleven o'clock, and we have all the shots we need. Besides, I don't want to risk another exploding volleyball. Let's pack up."

The small crowd of onlookers faded away as Frank joined in taking down the equipment, and Tammy collapsed onto a beach chair. Joe steered Chris to a spot a short distance from the others. "Uh, I was wondering," he said self-consciously, "do *you* think sports and dating mix?"

Chris laughed. "You bet. I don't go out that much, but not because I'm against it. Professional athletes don't usually have time for a great social life. There's the traveling and the training—"

As she was talking, two of the men's teams arrived to work out on one of the neighboring courts. Joe realized that one of them was George Ritt's team and that he was directing a very angry scowl their way. Chris saw him, too, and her words to Joe faded to a defeated sigh.

"I don't know what to do about Junior," she admitted.

"Junior?"

"His full name is George Ritt, Jr. Most of us call him Junior—behind his back. He has no reason to act like I'm his personal property. We've never even gone out. He gets on my nerves, but I can't help feeling sorry for him sometimes."

Joe stared in disbelief. *"Sorry? Why?"*

Chris grinned. "Wait till you meet George

senior. You will, if you stick around long enough."

Joe started to ask Chris what she meant, but their conversation was interrupted by a new voice. "Chris! Tammy!" A gray-haired woman strode across the sand toward them. She wore a gray sweatsuit, and a whistle hung from her neck. As she drew closer, Joe saw that the expression on her square face was very stern. He was glad when Frank walked over to join them.

"It's time for training now," the woman announced in a thick Eastern European accent. A volleyball from the men's court landed at her feet. She picked it up and expertly served it back to the players.

"Nadia," Chris said, a little flustered, "meet Joe Hardy and his brother, Frank. Guys, this is our trainer, Nadia Galinova."

Nadia nodded to each brother. Then she addressed the girls.

"Come. Now."

"But I want to take a swim."

Nadia fixed Tammy with a commanding stare. "There will be no swimming. You will be competing soon. Now come." Then she turned and rapidly strode back toward the clubhouse, paying no more attention to the group on the court. The girls reluctantly trailed along behind her. After a few steps Chris turned and waved mischievously to Joe.

"Tough lady," Frank commented, watching them go.

"You wouldn't believe *how* tough," agreed Chaplin as Joe and Frank helped him with his gear. "She was a top coach in regular volleyball in Czechoslovakia before she came here. Over there, her word was law, and it still is as far as she's concerned. You don't want to get on her bad side."

Joe stared after the three women. "What's so bad about mixing dating with sports?"

Chaplin smirked at Joe. "Interested in Chris, huh? Can't blame you. But watch out for Nadia. And Junior, too, while you're at it. He can be vicious, and his father is worse."

"Great," Joe remarked. "Nice bunch you have around here."

Frank straightened up from loading the larger camera into its hard case and wiped the sweat from his face with a towel. "Hey, Joe," he called, maintaining a casual expression. "Didn't Prindle tell us to check in for a new assignment after this?"

"Oh, right," Joe said, catching on immediately. "Okay if we go now, Ken?"

Ken gave his permission, and Joe followed Frank toward the far end of the surf club building. "What was that about?" he asked his brother as soon as they were out of earshot of the crew.

"We need to tell Prindle about the explosion," Frank explained. He took the incriminating pieces of rubber from his pocket. "It might give him some new ideas about who's doing this."

But when the boys found Prindle in his trailer and showed him the pieces of the exploded volleyball, the executive only turned a shade paler. "No one was hurt?" he repeated. "That's a break, anyway."

He then showed them a collection of fresh newspaper clippings piled on his desk. One of the headlines read, "Hi-Kick Contender Dies of Diabetic Attack."

"Whoever's doing this to the team must be planning to demand money before they'll stop— unless they're just plain crazy. I'm sure the company will pay—if it means no more trouble for the tour."

"But you can't pay someone when you don't know who or where they are," Frank pointed out. "Maybe there's a motive we don't know about yet."

"Yeah," said Joe. "And by the way, I was wondering if you could give us some background on Nadia Galinova. We ran into her today."

"She came here from Czechoslovakia twenty years ago," Prindle said, seemingly surprised at the switch in the conversation. "She used to coach regular volleyball, but when the beach version started getting popular, she was one of the first coaches to take it up. She coaches nearly all the top women players. Chris and Tammy, for instance—"

The phone on Prindle's desk rang, interrupting him.

"Prindle," he said into the receiver. Then his expression sharpened. "Yeah. Uh-huh. Oh, I see."

Frank and Joe watched as Prindle sat up straighter, his expression puzzled and upset. "B-but—" he stammered. Then his expression flattened, and he sagged back in his chair. "Okay. Thanks. Right."

He hung up the phone and took a deep breath.

"What was that about?" Joe asked. "More trouble?"

"That was the police," Prindle said resignedly. They want me to know that they've almost concluded that the cause of Osteen's death was hypoglycemic shock. Tests showed that his blood sugar took a nose dive just half an hour before he died."

"Then it wasn't murder," Frank said, surprised and oddly uneasy. "That's good news, right?"

"Not really." Prindle stared at the papers on his desk. Then he looked up at the boys. "The doctors said his blood sugar dropped. A diabetic's blood sugar drops only when he doesn't get enough sugar. But Peter had about half a gallon of Hi-Kick soda several hours before his death. And that was all he had."

Joe stared at him. "So?"

"So," Prindle said with a sigh, "Hi-Kick is loaded with sugar. Low blood sugar couldn't have killed him.

"The police told me their forensic department will be doing a complete tox screen on Osteen— a detailed analysis of his blood—just as a formality.

"And?" Joe demanded.

"And," said Frank, leaning toward Prindle, "you think it will prove Osteen was poisoned!"

Chapter

6

"YOU MEAN YOU can prove Osteen was poisoned?" Joe glanced at Frank for an explanation.

"Of course not!" Prindle ran a finger around the inside of his collar. "But I do know that Hi-Kick didn't kill him! Unfortunately, when this story comes out, everyone's going to *believe* our soda somehow killed him. It's a catastrophe!"

"What *did* kill him, then?" Frank asked. "Did someone put something in the drink? The police didn't find anything, though."

Prindle shook his head. "All they said was that the results of the tox screen would be ready tomorrow or the next day. Anyway, it doesn't matter. Even if the poor kid drank pure poison, people would still connect what happened with Hi-Kick. Believe me, I know. I've been in the promotion business over fifteen years."

"Maybe there's hope, though," Frank said, frowning. "After all, if Osteen *was* murdered, we need to know who did it and why. When the public finds out who did it and why, the bad press for Hi-Kick soda will have to die down."

Prindle appeared unconvinced. The three thought in silence for a moment until the office door opened and a burly man charged in. The reddish blond hair was receding on his head, but it grew thick on his powerful arms. His two small eyes were set close together, and his face was flushed with anger.

"Prindle, I want to talk to you!" he bellowed. Then he noticed Frank and Joe.

"Is one of you two named Hardy?" he demanded.

"Both of us are," Joe replied.

"Mr. Ritt," said Prindle, getting to his feet, "won't you come in?"

"Don't get smart with me," snarled the red-faced man. "These two young punks here—get rid of them, you hear me? Throw them out!"

"May I introduce George Ritt, Sr.," Prindle said to the Hardys. "George, Frank and Joe Hardy. Mr. Ritt's son is a player in the tournament, and George here takes a strong interest in his son's career."

"We met George junior this morning," said Frank.

"That's right, wise guy. He told me all about it." Mr. Ritt turned to Richard Prindle. "They were rifling through Peter Osteen's things, and

48

when my son called them on it, they started getting fresh with one of the girls. George took them to task for it—and I want them out of here."

"Wait a second," said Joe, getting out of his chair. "That's not the way it was."

"Relax, Joe," said Prindle, also getting up and stepping between Joe and George senior. "I'm not getting rid of anyone. George, your son has had problems with a lot of people around here, and it never seems to be his fault."

Mr. Ritt's face turned red. "Are you calling me a liar?"

"No," Prindle shouted in disgust. "But I don't take orders from you, and Frank and Joe are my employees. If any female player has a complaint, she can come to me herself."

"But—"

"George, I'd like to get back to work." Prindle walked to his office door and gestured for Ritt to leave. The older man glared at the Hardys for a long moment before starting out.

"And, George?" added Prindle. Ritt stopped on the trailer steps.

"Knock next time, will you?"

Ritt slammed the door hard enough to shake the trailer.

Prindle took a deep breath and returned to his desk. "Ritt inherited a lot of money when he was young and used it to make a fortune in real estate. Now he's retired and devotes his entire life to nothing but making his son the number-one player in the country. Believe me, you get to know some pushy parents in this business, but Ritt beats them all."

"*Is* Junior number one?" asked Frank.

Prindle smiled wanly. "He's young, and he has talent. But volleyball is a team game. The best teams stay together, learn from each other. Junior can't keep a partner. He's had some good ones, but sooner or later his dad drives them away."

"Who's he with now?" Frank prodded.

"Buzz Maestren," Prindle replied. "He's young, too, and wants to get onto the pro circuit. But I'll bet anything George'll drive him out."

He shook his head. "Osteen and Lenz were the surest bets to take the trophy from Conlin and Donahue—if anyone could."

Joe's ears perked up at this. "So Osteen was standing between Junior and the championship, in a way?" he asked.

Prindle blinked. "Hard to say. The tournament has just started. George junior hasn't even played yet."

"What's happening to Scooter?" Frank wanted to know.

"He's still in the competition," Prindle said. "He's hoping to line up another partner and come back later in the tournament."

"So," mused Frank, "we have a bunch of people who could benefit from Osteen's death. The Ritts, who want Junior to win the tournament,

Conlin and Donahue, who want to keep their place at the top—"

"And Nadia Galinova," Joe said, interrupting. "Chris said Nadia thought Osteen was a threat to Chris's career. Maybe Nadia would try to eliminate a threat like that."

"Now hold on a second," Prindle protested. "I never meant to imply for one second that Brad Conlin or Mark Donahue would—"

Joe held up a hand. "We're just going over people who might have motives. Besides, you'd be amazed how many murderers are 'wonderful people.'"

They heard a knock at the door just then and a voice calling, "Richard? Mark Donahue."

"Speak of the devil," Prindle murmured. Then he called, "Come in, Mark."

Mark and Brad Conlin walked in, saw the Hardys, and paused uncertainly. "Sorry," Mark said. "I didn't know you had company."

"That's okay, we're nearly finished here." Prindle motioned to Brad to close the door. At the appearance of the athletes, Prindle had become almost joyful. He seemed delighted to see the players and eager to know what was on their minds. Joe watched, amused. He knew that the promotion director's main job was to keep the competitors happy.

"Mark and Brad, meet Frank and Joe Hardy," Prindle said. They're volunteer workers. Now, what can I do for you guys?"

The players stared at Frank and Joe with more

interest. "Didn't one of you have a run-in with Junior this morning?" Brad Conlin asked.

"That was me," Joe admitted sheepishly. "I was looking for Chris Welles," he explained, "and the guy just attacked me."

Mark Donahue grimaced. "You're not the first one he's done that to. The guy's a stick of dynamite with a very short fuse. You never know what's going to set him off."

"He's like that with you guys, too?" Joe asked innocently.

Conlin laughed. "He doesn't try much. A lot of us are stronger than him. He did lay into Peter Osteen once, though, right in the locker room after he'd lost a match."

"Oh, yeah, I remember that," Donahue said. "Santa Barbara, right? Junior said Peter had palmed the ball—carried it instead of hitting it," he explained to the Hardys. "Junior protested to the ref, but the ref allowed the play. So poor Junior lost the match. It was beautiful."

"You sound like you don't like Junior much," Frank remarked.

Both players hesitated. "Well," Conlin said carefully, "he's not that bad. He just has a tendency to spout off when he ought to keep quiet. That time, he and Osteen got in a fight. The tournament officials had to come in and break it up themselves. I can still remember it. They kept on yelling at each other even when they were in separate rooms. Junior swore he'd get even."

"Right," Donahue said. "He was yelling stuff like, 'Nobody messes with George Ritt! I'll get you for this, Osteen!' "

Voicing both brothers' thoughts, Joe said in a low voice, "Sounds like a maniac."

Chapter

7

PRINDLE GLARED at the brothers. "Oh, come on," he said.

Ignoring him, Joe asked the athletes, "What happened then? Did Ritt and Osteen have any more problems?"

"Not that I know of," said Donahue. "Junior was put on probation for six months, but his dad got him out of it almost right away. After that, he and Osteen stayed away from each other." A funny expression fell over Donahue's face. "Why are we talking about this?" he asked. "Brad and I just came in to find out when we're doing the shoot for the Hi-Kick commercials."

"Yeah," said Conlin, only half-joking. "If Junior gets wind of what we've been saying, his dad'll have our necks."

"Don't worry." Joe made sure his laugh sounded casual. "I won't tell. I'm a fan."

Donahue grinned at Joe, then turned to Prindle. "So? When's the shoot?"

"Why don't you have a seat while I iron out a few details?" Prindle suggested. "We can go over the revised schedules, too. Oh, by the way, boys, take the rest of the day off. You deserve it."

Frank and Joe vacated their chairs. "Good luck in the games."

"Thanks," Donahue said. "The way this tournament's going, we can use all the luck we can get."

"Where to now?" Joe asked his brother as they stepped out of the trailer into the blinding sun.

"Our hotel room." Frank strode ahead across the parking lot. "I need to call Dad to ask him to check out George Ritt, Sr. I want to know if he has a record, or if anyone's ever sued him—that kind of thing."

"Good idea." Joe jogged to keep up with his brother. "Ask him to check out Nadia Galinova, too. She gives me the creeps."

Frank glanced at Joe. "That has nothing to do with Chris Welles, of course."

"I just want to cover all bases."

"Right." Frank couldn't resist teasing. "While I'm at it, maybe I should ask Dad to check whether Chris is married?"

Fifteen minutes after speaking to their dad, Frank and Joe left the hotel by the beach entrance to head for the surf's edge. In trunks and sandals, they'd walked about twenty yards when Joe held out an arm to stop his brother.

"Isn't that Mark Donahue out there?" Joe pointed toward the volleyball courts some distance to their right, where a tallish guy stood listening as a short, dark-haired man talked effusively with both hands and his mouth.

"Yeah. I recognize the other guy, too. He works for Frosty's competitors—uh, SuperJuice." Frank snapped his fingers. "Auerbach!"

"Right." Joe nodded. "Todd Auerbach."

As Joe spoke, Frank saw Auerbach glance in their direction, do a double take, and then abruptly shake Donahue's hand and walk off in the opposite direction toward the hotel parking lot.

"That was weird," said Joe. "Do you think he was trying to lure Donahue away from Frosty? So SuperJuice can sponsor Donahue instead?"

"It looks like it, doesn't it?" Frank agreed. "Maybe we should put Auerbach on our list of suspects."

"He stands to gain as much as the others if this tournament gets derailed," Joe agreed. He glanced over at the smooth, rolling waves. A blond male surfer was riding in on one of the crests, his legs bent perfectly and his board hardly moving. "But enough already," Joe added. "It's time to catch some rays."

As the brothers trudged past the gym area at the far end of the hotel, Joe glanced hopefully in the direction of the outdoor lounge. Chris Welles appeared just as he went by. She waved cheerfully at him.

"I thought you were warming up for your game," Joe called.

"We did." She strode across the sand toward him. "We just finished. Our match is at two o'clock this afternoon. Nadia wants us to jog on the beach, then go inside for a nap. Are you coming to the game?"

"You bet." Glancing over Chris's shoulder, Joe spotted Nadia Galinova watching them. He lowered his voice. "Maybe after the match I can take you for a victory dinner."

"What if we lose?" Chris asked, smiling.

"No problem," Frank chimed in. "Then he'll take you to a consolation dinner."

"Not that that's going to happen, of course," Joe assured her.

Chris laughed. "Sounds good," she said. "But it'll have to be early. I have a strict curfew."

"Great!" Joe's face brightened. "Are you going to run now? I'll walk you down the beach."

"You guys go ahead," Frank said. "I just remembered something I need to do at the hotel. Joe, I'll catch you later, either on the beach or at the hotel."

57

Joe barely glanced at his brother. "Ready, Chris?"

Chris winked mischievously at Frank, then set off with Joe. Frank could hear her chatting animatedly as the two of them crossed the sand to the water's edge. Smiling to himself, Frank heard a harsh voice just behind him.

"You. Tell your brother to mind his own business. Otherwise, there could be trouble."

Frank turned, already knowing he would see Nadia Galinova standing behind him. "What kind of trouble?" he demanded.

The coach didn't answer. She folded her arms across her chest, and her face grew even more stony and forbidding.

"Stay away from Chris and Tammy or you will be very, very sorry," she said forcefully. Then she turned back toward the gym.

Frank understood what Joe meant when he'd said that Galinova gave him the creeps.

Frank called his father again and added Todd Auerbach's name to the list of those he wanted investigated. Then he called Richard Prindle to describe the scene he and Joe had witnessed between Mark Donahue and Todd Auerbach.

"He's been sniffing around since we got set up here," Prindle said, annoyed. "He'd love to cause trouble."

"But you already have all the players under contract, right?" said Frank.

"Yes, but if the tournament is scrapped, the

contracts are worthless, and Auerbach could sign up anyone he wants for endorsements. He's probably making sure they keep him in mind—just in case.''

Prindle paused, then blurted out, ''I sure hope you boys get this whole business straightened out soon. I'm getting worn out.''

''Don't worry,'' Frank assured him. ''We're looking forward to winding it up so we can start our vacation, too.''

Meanwhile, Joe Hardy had finally found the perfect spot to lay out his towel—just above the high-water mark. He stripped off his T-shirt and walked the few feet to the water. The surf was low, and the water not very cold. Some small children were splashing and laughing in the shallower waves.

Joe had left Chris and Tammy to their jogging, but all he could think about was dinner with Chris as he waded out into the ocean. He was only waist-deep even after he'd walked more than fifty yards. The wet sand was firm under his feet, and the chill of the water contrasted perfectly with the heat from the sun.

Joe dived forward and began swimming farther out. Soon he could barely hear the laughter of the children playing. He rolled onto his back and closed his eyes against the sun. His mind wandered to the Osteen case and what they'd learned about Peter's death so far.

Plenty of people, it seemed, had a reason to

wish Peter Osteen out of the picture. But were any of them capable of killing a person? Joe let the images of Nadia, George Ritt and his son, and Auerbach run through his mind. He really couldn't imagine any of them brutally ending a young man's life. Besides, whoever was causing the trouble seemed interested in more than Osteen. After all, the threatening phone calls had been made to plenty of people, and Chaplin's equipment had been vandalized.

It felt as if he'd been drifting a lifetime when Joe suddenly heard someone splash up beside him. It took Frank long enough to get here, he thought idly, not bothering to open his eyes.

An angry voice jarred him out of his pleasant mood.

"I warned you to stay away from Chris, and you came down to the beach with her. I guess I'm going to have to teach you a lesson."

It was Junior.

Instinctively, Joe swung around in the water to face his enemy. Glancing over Junior's shoulder, he realized Frank was nowhere in sight. But standing on the shore George senior was watching them.

"Okay, just a second—" Joe said, stalling.

Junior didn't feel like waiting. He looped one strong arm around Joe's throat and yanked hard.

Joe was being pulled under!

Chapter

8

DON'T PANIC, Joe told himself as Junior forced his head under. He thrashed helplessly, trying to pry Junior's hands loose from his throat. But he couldn't do it. Junior was too strong for him. Joe needed air—right then!

Think of something! he thought wildly as the pressure on his lungs grew more painful. But the athlete's grip remained tight on his throat. Joe started feeling dizzy, and his legs stopped kicking. Junior was going to kill him, he realized dimly. Gradually, unable to resist, Joe started to relax.

As his body began to go limp, Joe sensed that Junior was relaxing, too. He willed himself to stay awake and wait for an opening. Just when Junior seemed about to let go, Joe gathered his strength and exploded. Jabbing his elbow in

Junior's stomach just below his rib cage, Joe pushed him down and away as hard as he could.

Abruptly, the powerful arm loosened its grip, and Joe bobbed free to the surface to inhale a lungful of air. He was still gasping when Junior broke the surface nearby.

"You don't own her, Junior," Joe said hotly, treading water and glaring at his attacker.

The volleyball player's eyes popped wide open. "Don't call me that!" He took a slow-motion punch through the water at Joe's head. Joe easily avoided it.

"Watch out, George. You're out of your depth. I don't have my back turned now."

"I'll show you—" Junior plunged toward Joe, but Joe was more maneuverable in the water and had no trouble staying out of reach. As Joe turned to swim back toward the beach, Junior grabbed hold of Joe's left ankle and twisted it. Joe went with the motion, and rolled over on his back. Kicking out with his free leg, he caught the athlete in the jaw with his heel. Junior fell back, stunned.

I should leave him here, Joe thought angrily. Even though he was sure Junior wouldn't do the same for him, Joe knew he'd have to save him from drowning. Joe threw an arm around Junior's chest and slowly pulled him toward shore. He let him go when he could stand, and the athlete staggered in behind him on his own rubbery legs.

It didn't surprise Joe to see George Ritt, Sr., storming toward him.

"You could have drowned my boy out there!" the older man was shouting. "I'll have you arrested for assault!"

Still trying to catch his breath, Joe glanced at Ritt and shook his head. "Your son started this," he said, checking for witnesses. A girl and two boys were watching them with expressions of alarm.

He turned back to Mr. Ritt. "I was just defending myself."

"Oh, yeah?" growled the elder Ritt. "We'll see what the police have to say about that. In any case, you'll be getting the bill for his hospital costs. And if he loses his match tomorrow, we'll sue!"

"What's going on here?" To Joe's great relief, Frank was approaching. He took in Junior, who was still gasping as he made his way to the shore.

"Don't tell me *Junior's* been acting up again," Frank said loudly. To Joe's satisfaction, Junior's jaw muscles tightened, and he glowered at Frank.

"Now you've done it," Joe commented. "If he tries to drown someone who only speaks to Chris Welles, who knows what he'd do to someone who calls him Junior."

"I wasn't trying to drown you," Junior growled. "Just knock some respect into you, that's all. I'm not a murderer, no matter what—"

"Shut your mouth!" Mr. Ritt's voice lashed

out like a whip, and his son stopped in midsentence. "Come on, George. Time to go." But before they left, he gave Joe a long, cold stare.

"Don't think you've seen the last of us," he said. "Nobody messes with the Ritts."

Joe was looking from son to father, wondering what George had started to say before his father interrupted him. "Did Peter Osteen mess with the Ritts?" he asked abruptly. "Is that why he's dead now?"

Neither man answered. The older Ritt stared stonily at the Hardys, but Joe thought he noted a slight change in his expression.

Before anyone said anything more, Joe heard a dune buggy approaching. The group turned to see Vern Elliott, the assistant film director, and his boss, Ken Chaplin, approaching in a red buggy with a blue-and-gold Hi-Kick logo painted on the hood. Chaplin held a large camera on his lap, while Vern drove. Joe wondered if the dune buggy was a prop for a promotional film.

"What's going on, guys?" Chaplin shouted over the noise of the engine. "Is Ritt giving you a hard time?"

"Mind your own business, Chaplin," Ritt growled. "You want to keep your job, right? I know you need the money."

Vern cut the engine, and Chaplin deliberately set his camera on the floor of the vehicle and slowly climbed out onto the sand. "Are you threatening me, Ritt?" he asked, standing up to the retired magnate. "It's none of your business whether I need the money or how much I need. Richard Prindle pays my salary, not you. Or maybe you're trying to do to me what you did to Chuck Herrick last year."

George Ritt's face turned reddish purple. "That's slander, Chaplin!" he roared. "No one ever proved we did anything to Herrick. I'd take you to court for that, if you weren't such a loser that it wouldn't be worth it. How much do you owe for your gambling debts, anyway? I hear it's so much you'll be doing hack work for the rest of your life."

Chaplin's jaw was clenched, but he remained in tight control as Ritt collected his son and left without another word.

"You were sure right to warn me about Junior," Joe told Chaplin when the Ritts were out of earshot. "He attacked me out in the water because he saw me walking on the beach with Chris."

Chaplin nodded, acting very tired all of a sudden. "Yeah. Steer clear of the Ritts. That's still my advice."

"What happened between you two in the past?" Frank asked.

Chaplin shrugged ruefully. "I was hired to shoot a documentary last year for the Beach Volleyball Federation, to publicize the sport. Old man Ritt instantly started giving me grief over it. He accused me of not devoting enough film time to his son. He said that since Junior was going to be the game's top player, I owed him more exposure than the other players. It started to irritate me, so I finally told him that if he pestered me any more I'd cut his son out of the film altogether."

Joe gave a low whistle. "I bet that went over big," he said.

"Right." Chaplin backed up onto the sand as a wave lapped at his canvas shoe. "Next thing I knew, the federation called me on the carpet and told me I was through. They said they couldn't have people offending their major backers."

"What about this Chuck Herrick you mentioned?" Frank asked.

Chaplin seemed taken aback. "I'm not supposed to talk about this stuff. Anyway, we've got to get ready to shoot the women's match soon. Are you guys assigned to me again today?"

Ignoring the question, Frank assessed Chaplin's reaction. "You're still scared of Ritt, aren't you?"

Anger flickered across the filmmaker's face. "Sure I'm scared," he said. "The man has a very long, strong arm. Listen, some of us have work to do. See you two later at the court."

He climbed back in the buggy and was driven off. "Well, I don't know who's more suspicious of us now," Joe said, picking up his towel and briskly drying himself off. "Ritt senior or

Chaplin. We haven't been acting much like lowly assistants lately."

"Maybe not," replied Frank. "But at least we're getting some information. I want to find out more about this Chuck Herrick. I wonder what Ritt did to him that was never proved."

"Maybe Chris knows about it," Joe suggested. "I could ask her at dinner."

Frank grinned. "Sure you don't want to be off duty tonight? She might not like being pumped for information. And you might make her suspicious."

"I don't like not being able to tell her who I really am. You think there's any chance of wrapping up this case before the tournament's over?"

"Only if we quit lazing around on the beach and get back to work." Frank grinned at his brother. "In fact, I'm going to skip my swim and go ask Prindle a few questions. Like what kind of gambling problems Chaplin has. And what he knows about Ritt getting Chaplin fired. Then we need to be at the court for Chris and Tammy's match."

As they talked, Frank and Joe started toward the hotel parking lot. "You think Chaplin was telling the truth about Ritt firing him?" Joe asked.

"Who knows? He hates Ritt enough to stretch the truth, that's obvious. By the way, I called Dad from the hotel and asked him to run a check on Todd Auerbach. And—oh, yes—I had a wonderful chat with Nadia Galinova.''

"I'll bet that was fun," said Joe with a laugh. "Did she say she'd put a contract out on me if I didn't leave Chris alone?"

"Not in so many words," said Frank. "But I bet you're right—she is hiding something."

"Do you think she could have had something to do with Osteen's death?" Joe asked in surprise.

"The motive is really weak—you don't kill somebody just to keep your athletes from getting distracted."

"Not if you're sane. But judging from what Chaplin and Prindle have said about her, Galinova seems a little out of touch with reality. Like she's still in the old country, where she can crack the whip."

Frank nodded. "Let's see what Prindle can tell us," he said. "Then we'll have just enough time to grab some lunch before Chris and Tammy's match. Who are they playing, anyway?"

Joe shrugged. "It doesn't matter. Chris and Tammy will roll right over them. Like a machine."

Frank grinned at his brother. "Just don't go shouting advice to them from behind the court. That's all they need—some would-be boyfriend getting them disqualified."

"Don't worry." Joe's smile gleamed against his new layer of tan. "The last thing Chris needs is my advice."

When the brothers reached Prindle's trailer at the edge of the parking lot, Joe pushed the door open, forgetting to knock, and the two brothers stepped inside.

Prindle wasn't there. Someone else was sitting at his desk, leafing through stacks of papers. Todd Auerbach!

Chapter

9

"WHAT ARE YOU doing here?" Frank asked, astounded.

"What do you mean?" Auerbach seemed to be puzzled. Then his face brightened. "Oh! You mean going through Richard's things! Don't worry, boys, he knows all about it. Can I help you with something? You need a work schedule or what?"

"Wait a minute," said Joe, stepping closer. "You work for SuperJuice, right? I don't think Mr. Prindle would want you poking around his desk. You'd better stop. Right now."

Auerbach glared disdainfully at Joe. "Why don't you take a hike?" he said smoothly. "Let the grown-ups do their jobs."

"Fine." Joe's voice shook with anger. "I'll take a hike. Straight to the police."

Auerbach's grin faded. "Look, boys," he said icily. "I don't like being threatened."

"Then why don't you leave?" said Frank, standing beside his brother and presenting an obvious threat to Auerbach.

Auerbach blinked several times. Then he stood up, backed around the desk chair, and edged toward the door. "Fine," he said. "No need to flex your muscles. But believe me—your boss will hear about the way you treat guests in his office!"

"You bet he'll hear about it," Joe called after Auerbach as he hustled out the door. "The minute we find him."

The door slammed, and the brothers glanced at each other, perplexed. "What was he looking for?"

"Beats me," Joe answered. "He's got a lot of nerve, though, just walking in when no one's around."

"There's a list of players' phone numbers and addresses here on top," Frank said, picking up a piece of paper. "And some contracts. Maybe he was looking for loopholes to get the athletes out of their agreements with Frosty. I bet SuperJuice wants to get into the beach volleyball business, too."

"He'll probably contact the players at home, in private," Joe agreed. "I wish we'd asked him a few questions while we had him here."

Frank shook his head. "A guy like that would have a reasonable answer for whatever we asked him. Anyway, he'd start wondering pretty quick why a couple of gofers wanted to know so much. He looks smart, even if he is slime."

"If he's so smart, why doesn't he come up with his own promotion idea? Why steal Frosty's?" Joe asked.

"Good question. Another thing I wonder, is he the kind of person who'd murder to get what he wanted?"

"While we're here, why don't you call Dad to see if he has the info on our suspects yet," Joe said.

It took only five minutes for Frank to listen to all the information his father had called up on his computer regarding the murder suspects.

"First of all, he says George Ritt did really well with his real estate business," Frank began telling Joe. "He's a major big shot in southern California. No arrest record, but he's been sued a few times for shoddy business practices. He has a reputation for being a very tough businessman."

"Big surprise," Joe commented dryly. "What about Auerbach?"

"Nothing on him yet. No federal record or anything. Nadia Galinova's a different story, though. Dad says she's still a registered alien after almost twenty years in this country. She's never applied for American citizenship, which is a little unusual but not unheard of. No criminal record for her, either."

"Great. That gives us just about nothing new to work on." Joe sighed, then said, "I'm starved. Let's go eat. We can tell Prindle what happened when we see him at the tournament."

As the brothers left the office, they saw Vern hastily unlocking a padlock on the film trailer door. "Hi, Vern," Frank said in a friendly voice. "How's the setup going?"

"We're running late," the middle-aged man said gruffly. "And now, after opening this lock, I have to fiddle with this dumb security system."

"What's wrong with it?" Frank approached the film office, watching intently as Vern punched in a code on an expensive-looking switch box next to the door.

"Nothing's wrong with it," Vern grumbled absentmindedly. "I just have to remember the code every time I need a lousy roll of film. Chaplin tried to make the code something I'd always remember," he said. "But I still have to think before I punch it in."

Vern entered the office, and Frank noted that the security system Chaplin had bragged about consisted only of an alarm system and a single padlock.

"See you at the court this afternoon." Frank called up to Vern from the bottom of the steps. "I was hoping I could get a look at all your equipment. I'm kind of interested in film myself."

"You'll have to ask Chaplin." Vern's voice floated out of the trailer's dim interior. "Can't be too security minded around here."

*　　*　　*

"Vern acted like he didn't quite trust us," Joe observed as he and Frank finished their sandwiches.

The restaurant was nearly empty. Frank figured nearly everyone had gone to watch the women's match. They'd have to hurry if they were going to get to work on time.

"They *did* have some equipment ruined. How can they be sure we didn't do it?"

As they left the snack bar and headed for the tournament down the beach, Frank glanced wistfully at the rolling waves. Two full days there and he hadn't been in the ocean once. It was getting ridiculous. He felt like jumping in and swimming out far enough to escape his frustrations.

"We're just in time," Joe said as they approached the near end of the court. Frank nodded. The bleachers were overflowing with people, and tense-looking tournament officials were rushing everywhere. The bad publicity of the day before hadn't hurt attendance any.

"There you are!" Frank heard Prindle call. "Just in time. Frank, you'll be retrieving balls on the far side, over there. Joe, I want you right here. You'll both have a perfect view of everything that goes on, and you can keep your cover intact, too."

"Thanks, Mr. Prindle," Joe said. "Listen, we have something we need to tell you about—"

"Sorry, boys. Can't talk now. Tell me after the match."

Prindle hurried off. Joe shrugged at his

brother. Then he beamed at someone over Frank's shoulder.

Frank turned and saw Chris peeling off her warm-ups and smiling back at Joe. Nadia Galinova was standing at one side of center court, glaring at the boys. Frank felt a chill run down his spine at the look on the coach's face. He wondered what had happened in her past to make her so hateful.

"I see you've been spotted," Frank said ironically to Joe as he started toward the far end of the court. "Good luck catching balls."

"Right." Joe ran a hand through his hair to get it out of his eyes. A strong breeze had started blowing in off the ocean. He wondered how much the wind would affect the competition.

With mock salutes, the two Hardys took up their positions, facing each other across the court. Frank watched as Chris and Tammy jogged in place to warm up. Then he looked over at the other team—a redhead nearly as tall as Tammy, and a slightly shorter, stockier brunette with a very determined expression.

The loudspeakers announced the players, the audience burst out in loud applause, and the match began. It started out so exciting that Frank forgot everything but the game.

Chris and Tammy were ahead one game to none when Frank noticed a high, whining noise from somewhere nearby. He glanced around, trying to locate the source of the sound.

It must be the wind blowing past those guy wires, he decided, eyeing the huge Hi-Kick bottles at the corners of the court that were held in place by heavy metal cable. The cables were held down by anchors that looked like giant hooks screwed partway into the sand. The hooks looked as secure as granite.

But Frank was wrong. As Tammy prepared to serve and Chris stood poised near the net, Frank heard a loud metallic twang at his left. Out of the corner of his eye he saw one of the giant Hi-Kick models flap free. He spun to his left just in time to see one cable anchor tear itself free from the ground and fly into the air, straight at Chris!

Chapter

10

JOE ALSO SAW the heavy anchor flying through the air. "Chris! Duck!" he yelled, charging forward. Chris whirled around in confusion as Joe ran across the court to smash into Chris with his best running back tackle. He was just in time to knock her flat as the anchor flew over her and fell back to the sand.

As everyone screamed, Joe stayed where he was and tried to calm Chris. He could feel her trembling.

"What happened?" she whispered to Joe as all the officials descended on them.

"The cable and anchor," Joe said falteringly. "They pulled loose. Someone must have—"

"Oh, no!" Chris covered her face with her hands. "Not again."

"Are you all right, Chris?" It was Richard

Prindle, with Nadia Galinova, Tammy, and Frank right behind him.

"Yes. I think so," she said shakily. "I just don't understand—"

"It was an accident with those stupid bottles," Nadia interrupted furiously. "I told you they weren't safe, Mr. Prindle. But you had to advertise, you said. Well, you might have just lost another valuable athlete because of your greed—"

"Please, Nadia," Chris interrupted. "I don't think there was anything wrong with the anchors. I think this was deliberate."

Prindle stared at her, slightly green. The television news crews began crowding in, and Prindle leapt to his feet to order them off the court.

"Come, Chris," Nadia ordered, helping her up. "We'll take you to the hospital."

"No," Chris said as she got to her feet and brushed herself off. "I want to finish the game, Nadia." Her eyes went to Tammy, who hung back, waiting to talk to her friend. "That is, if it's okay with my partner."

Tammy nodded mutely. As the teammates walked over to the television cameras to announce their decision, they were trailed by a fuming coach.

Frank and Joe made their way to where the anchor had pulled out of the sand.

"It doesn't make sense," Joe said over the noise of the crowd's cheers as they learned that the match would go on. "This kind of cable and its anchor are made to last for years. All of a sudden they can't hold an inflated model up for two or three days?"

"Someone sabotaged the cable, no doubt about it," Frank agreed, straightening up. "The question is, did they do it just to disrupt the tourney?"

"I can't wait till we catch this guy. I have a long list of questions I want to throw at him," Joe said.

The brothers were unable to investigate further because the match was about to start again. Prindle was motioning wildly for them to take their places at either end of the court.

The crowd belonged completely to Chris for the remainder of the match, and Joe proudly witnessed her team win. After she and Tammy had shaken hands with the competition, Joe jogged over to ask her when she'd be ready to go out and celebrate.

"Pick me up at Tammy's in two hours," she said. She gave him the address and directions.

"Thanks." Joe backed away to let other well-wishers approach her.

Joe saw Junior beaming at Chris from the edge of the crowd. He was so tall, he didn't need to move closer to be able to see her. "How about celebrating with me tonight?" he yelled to Chris.

"Sorry, George. I have other plans," Chris called back.

As Joe passed Junior he gave him a slap on

the back. "That's the way it goes, George," he said.

Junior was ready to fight right then, but for some reason he wheeled around and walked away instead, brushing past people without noticing them.

"Hey, Chris and Tammy, way to go!" Joe saw Brad Conlin, Mark Donahue, and Scooter Lenz approaching from the direction of the bleachers. He guessed most of the players had watched this match. Frank brought up the rear, holding the winning volleyball.

"Thanks, guys. Hi, Scooter," Chris said, her smile faltering for an instant. "Thanks for coming. I'll show up at all your games, too."

The male players laughed. Tammy asked, "Scooter, have you found a new partner yet?"

The others went silent as Lenz stared down at the sand. "Haven't come up with anyone yet," he admitted. "It's kind of hard to replace Osteen, you know? He had guts."

Joe moved closer to Scooter, and Frank joined the two of them as they were shunted aside by eager officials, Chaplin's film crew, and the television news crews.

"Scooter, you said you wanted us to help out about Peter," Joe said, keeping his voice low.

Scooter nodded.

"Well, we're still working on it," Frank said gently. "But we have a couple of questions. We saw the machine Peter used to monitor his blood sugar. He did that regularly, right?"

"Before every match and workout," Lenz replied. "He'd had diabetes since he was a kid so he knew the ropes. Doing the kind of exercise he did, the amount of sugar in his blood could go way up or down in a short period of time. If it ever went too far in either direction, he'd— well, he'd die. So he kept fresh fruit by his locker to keep his sugar level high enough. He also carried a kit with insulin and hypodermic needles."

"The insulin would lower his blood sugar level, right?" asked Frank.

"Right," Scooter replied. "Just before yesterday's match, he took out one of those syringes and gave himself a shot. 'This is to make up for all that sweet Hi-Kick soda we're going to have to drown ourselves in on the court,' he said to me. He stayed away from the fruit that day for the same reason." Scooter's voice faltered.

"Thanks, man," Joe said, patting him on the shoulder. To make Scooter feel better, he added, "I guess he hadn't counted on such a long, hard match in such hot weather." But he knew Frank was thinking the same thing he was. It was more likely that someone had been out to get Osteen, and that was why he had died.

Two hours later Joe arrived in slacks, jacket, and tie at the front door of Tammy's cottage. "You sure look handsome," Chris teased, answering the door in a pretty silk blouse and skirt. "Are you selling something door to door?"

"Just giving stuff away." Joe brought a bouquet of flowers out from behind his back. Pleased, Chris gave him a kiss on the cheek.

"I know a perfect seafood place on the beach," she said. "And since you're new here, you have to go where I say."

"Sounds perfect," he said.

The road to the restaurant wound among spectacular cliffs and canyons, past towering palm trees, and lush tropical flowers. They caught an occasional glimpse of the Pacific Ocean between the trees. "Sometimes I wonder why my parents ever decided to live in Bayport," Joe admitted, admiring the view, "when they could have picked a place as great as this."

"But then you'd have grown up as just another California surfer boy," Chris teased, "and I would never have noticed you."

Joe liked the seafood restaurant right away because Chris was known there, and they were led to the very best, most private table on the open-air terrace.

Joe dug into his order of shrimp and steak and enjoyed the sight of Chris eating hungrily.

"This food is great!" she said.

"Hey, that's my line," he joked. "I think you're the only girl I've ever met who can out-eat me."

"Yeah, and that worries me," she admitted cheerfully. "I mean, I'm not going to play beach volleyball all my life. What'll happen to me if I stop playing but my appetite stays?"

"You can always become a food writer," he suggested. "Then when you get fat everyone will think you're just doing your job."

Chris laughed. Then she stopped abruptly.

"What's wrong?" asked Joe.

Chris didn't answer for a moment. She finally relaxed again and smiled shakily at Joe. "Nothing. I saw Junior's dad over there, and I was afraid Junior was with him. But it looks like he's alone."

Joe glanced through a large window into the interior of the restaurant. He spotted Ritt in a booth, talking to someone who looked familiar. Joe realized with a jolt that it was Todd Auerbach.

"What's he doing with Auerbach?" he muttered.

"Oh, Auerbach's been trying to get us to break our Frosty contracts and sign endorsement deals with SuperJuice," Chris said calmly. "George senior is Junior's manager, so Auerbach is probably giving him a big sell."

Joe nodded, but noted that Ritt was doing the talking. "By the way, I wanted to ask you—do you know Chuck Herrick?"

Chris was obviously surprised. "Sure. But where did you hear about him? He hasn't played for a year now."

"Ken Chaplin said something nasty about the

Ritts and Chuck Herrick. It got Ritt all huffed up. What's that about, anyway?"

Chris got serious. "I don't know if I should talk about it because nobody knows anything for sure." Then she smiled. "Well, I owe you one after you saved my life today. This is strictly rumor, understand?"

"Understood," Joe replied.

"Chuck was a good player, but last year, just before a match with Junior and his partner, he suddenly got real sick. He had to go to the hospital. Of course, he had to forfeit the match and Junior won. People thought 'someone' might have put something into his pregame food, but nothing could be proved.

"Then, right after the tournament," Chris continued, "Junior's partner had a big argument with Junior and walked out on him. No one knows what it was about. He just cleared out and left the circuit. He won't even talk to his old volleyball buddies on the phone. It was all kind of suspicious, but no one's ever been accused or anything."

Chris checked her watch and smiled at Joe. "Nine o'clock. I'd better be getting home," she said, "or Nadia will ground me for the rest of the year."

Joe asked for the check, paid it, and the two of them left the terrace for the inside of the restaurant.

"I don't think they've seen us," Chris whispered, referring to Auerbach and George Ritt.

"Let's try to sneak out without their noticing us. I'm really not in the mood for small talk."

"Fine with me," Joe said, and led her the long way around the booths.

As they passed the rest rooms on the way out, Chris said, "I'll meet you outside, okay? My hair could use a touch-up after all it's been through today."

Joe wandered out to the parking lot to wait for Chris as she'd asked. Outside, his eyes fell on a luxury convertible parked near the building. A gold monogram on the driver's door read "G.R."

This must be Ritt senior's, Joe thought derisively. He ran a hand along the smooth paint, admiring the car in spite of himself. The top was down, and he could see the all-leather interior, the CD player, the cruise control.

It occurred to Joe that this might be the perfect opportunity to do a little sleuthing. He made sure no one was watching. The car appeared to be empty, but Joe wondered if something incriminating might be hidden in the glove compartment or in the trunk.

He tried the glove compartment. It wasn't locked. Popping the door open, Joe found a sheaf of receipts and papers. He rifled through them.

The receipts were all made out to George Ritt. Most of them were restaurant, gas, and garage receipts, but one bill stood out. It was for a small-size container of something called Biodane, bought at the Meadowlark Garden Center somewhere around Laguna Beach. Joe tried to imagine George Ritt gardening, but that seemed impossible. Joe stuffed the receipt in his pocket and returned the rest of the papers to the glove compartment. He turned away just as Chris appeared at the entrance to the restaurant. She walked out to join him and tucked her arm through his.

"Like the car?" she asked.

"Not my style."

"Mine, neither." She sighed. "I hate to say this, but I'd better get back pronto."

"I know," Joe said. "Maybe we can do this again sometime. When you have no curfew."

Chris smiled and squeezed Joe's arm. "I'd like that."

They began the drive back up the beautiful Coast Highway in silence, lost in their own thoughts. "I wish Frank could see this," Joe said after a while. "He was looking forward to rediscovering California, and he's hardly left the hotel. Tonight he's having an early dinner and watching a movie on TV."

"Poor guy. We'll invite both of you over to Tammy's sometime," Chris said with a smile. "That way he can experience how the natives live."

Joe turned off the Coast Highway and onto the narrow road where Tammy lived. Tammy's cottage was in a quiet neighborhood with no streetlights along the winding canyon road.

"I had a great time," Joe said after he'd walked Chris to the front door.

"Me, too," Chris replied. "Let's—"

A loud *thump* sounded from inside the house and stopped Chris's next comment. It was quickly followed by a muffled cry.

Then Tammy's voice rang out in the evening air.

"No!"

Joe and Chris stared at each other.

Tammy was in trouble!

Chapter
11

"WAIT HERE," Joe snapped. He found the door unlocked and charged in. Tammy was kneeling on the living room floor, struggling with a man standing above her in a baggy gray sweatsuit and a rubber mask that covered his whole head. The man had Tammy in a choke hold with her right arm bent up sharply behind her back. Another man in a similar getup stood nearby doubled over and gasping.

Joe lowered his shoulder and drove it into Tammy's attacker at waist level. The impact made the man let Tammy go, and she flew forward onto the floor. Her attacker was thrown off balance long enough for Joe to throw a short but potent uppercut punch to his jaw. The man stumbled back, dazed.

Joe turned toward the second man, who had

just managed to stand upright. Backing away from Joe, he croaked, "Let's split!" and turned for the door.

Joe started after him, but just as he reached out to grab him, a tremendous blow fell on the back of his head. The room exploded with stars as Joe pitched forward, crashing into a low table that collapsed under his weight. Through a haze of pain, he saw something bright and hard fall on the floor beside him and heard the assailants race out the door.

A car engine roared to life outside as Chris raced in.

"Tammy!" she gasped, ignoring the squeal of tires as the attackers made their getaway. "Joe! What—how—"

"Don't worry about me," Tammy said, her voice hoarse from the stranglehold she'd just been subjected to. "See about Joe."

"I'm okay." Joe carefully disentangled himself from the splintered table. He stared down, still feeling a little dizzy, and saw that the hard, shiny object was a volleyball trophy. The intruder must have hit him over the head with it.

"Good thing that trophy was kind of tinny," he said, "or I'd be in a lot worse shape."

Chris led Joe to the kitchen table and sat him down on one of the wooden chairs, then began carefully examining the back of his head. Tammy joined them.

"No blood," Chris announced to Joe. "But you'll have a nasty bump there for a few days."

"I've had worse. Sorry about the table," Joe added. "Tammy, what happened?"

Tammy's eyes widened as she started to talk. "I was sitting here, listening to music," she said, "when the door burst open and those two goons stormed in and grabbed me. I think they were trying to kidnap me. I kicked one in the stomach, but the other one got a choke hold on me. And that was when you showed up."

"Do you have any idea who they were?"

"None." Tammy shook her head firmly. "I was too busy fighting them to worry about who they were."

Joe sighed. "Where's the phone?" he asked.

"Right there," Tammy asked, indicating the kitchen counter. "Why?"

"I'm calling the police."

Tammy groaned. "Prindle will murder us!"

"Tammy, you were assaulted," Joe said sharply. "This isn't the kind of thing to cover up."

"But, Joe," Chris said tentatively, "there's a clause in our endorsement contracts that says if we defame the company in any way—you know, by causing a scandal or attracting any kind of negative attention—the Frosty Company doesn't have to pay us anymore. Tammy would be in big trouble, income-wise, if her contract was broken."

"Yeah," said Tammy, lifting her chin. "Besides, Nadia would have my head if she knew I hadn't locked my door."

Joe frowned. He didn't like the idea of not reporting the incident. What if the men came back, or something similar happened again? He knew he'd blame himself.

"All right," he said at last. "How about this? We'll call them and give them just the plain facts without the lurid details. They can draw their own conclusions. And I think I can get them not to leak any of it to the papers."

At last Tammy agreed and Joe made the call. Ten minutes later two squad cars pulled up in front of the cottage. Two detectives and two uniformed officers knocked at the front door and entered. One of the men was Detective Dan O'Boyle. He introduced his partner as Detective Ericsson, and they joined the group at the kitchen table while the uniformed officers searched for clues.

After Tammy had given her brief account of what happened, Detective O'Boyle asked Joe, "Did you notice their car when you drove up?"

"I'm afraid not. I must have seen it, but it didn't register. There aren't any streetlights, so I couldn't see much of anything."

Detective Ericsson asked Joe a few more questions about the attackers' height and weight, and then the two detectives stood up. "We don't have much, do we?" said O'Boyle. "No good descriptions, no prints, no license number, nothing. But I have the feeling that someone around here doesn't like volleyball players very much."

"It could be, I guess," Joe said uncomfortably.

"Anyone want to add anything?" O'Boyle looked at Tammy, Chris, and Joe in turn. None of them spoke. O'Boyle coughed. "You, young ladies, lock your doors from now on. Good night."

After the police had left, Joe said to Chris, "I'd better go, too. Will you be all right?"

Chris nodded, and Tammy bragged, "They don't scare me. If there had been just one of them, I could have taken him, easy."

"I bet." Joe saluted her with a smile. "Call if there's a problem, okay?"

"We will." Chris got up from the table and walked him to the front door. "Thanks, Joe," she said as he walked outside. "For everything."

Joe hurried to his car, a goofy grin plastered across his face.

It was nearly eleven o'clock when Frank was startled awake by the sound of angry voices shouting. Still confused by sleep, he thought at first that the sounds were coming from the television set in his room.

Finally he realized that the voices were coming from somewhere outside, drifting through his open door that led to the terrace. He strained his ears to try to identify the voices. One of them sounded like Nadia Galinova's!

After getting off the bed, Frank moved silently

toward the open door, listening to Nadia's angry voice shouting at some unknown victim. Now a low voice rumbled an answer. Frank realized that that voice belonged to George Ritt, Sr.

No matter how hard he tried, Frank couldn't decipher what the older man was saying. But Nadia's voice came loud and clear in reply: *"No! I cannot!"*

Another man's voice joined in, speaking more softly, apparently urging Nadia to be quieter. The voices started to move away, growing softer. Frustrated, Frank leaned over the rail.

He spotted three people walking close along the wall of the hotel, their backs to Frank. Ritt and Nadia were recognizable to him—the other man was not.

He leaned farther out to get a better look. As he did, the trio reached the corner of the building and turned. Curious about the identity of the second man, Frank slipped over the second-story railing and dropped to the sand below. Moving swiftly but silently, he raced after the little group, keeping close to the wall.

The other man wasn't Junior because he was much too short.

At the corner of the building, Frank pressed against the wall and cautiously peered around it. The trio was on the way to one of the parking lots that served the beach crowds—now deserted in the night. Frank saw that Ritt had a grip on Galinova's arm just above the elbow. The woman was dragging her feet, appearing to be afraid as she tried to pull away from his powerful grasp.

Then Frank heard the second man speak. "Take it easy, George."

The voice was familiar, but Frank couldn't place it. Just then the three of them moved into the bright circle of light from a street lamp. Frank stared. The other man was Todd Auerbach!

Ritt and Auerbach—what was the connection, Frank wondered. And what did they want with Galinova?

Not wanting to be discovered, Frank turned and started noiselessly back. He was so involved in his own thoughts that he failed to hear someone moving up behind him until the last second.

By then it was too late. Frank started to turn just as something heavy and solid crashed into his skull. He dropped to the ground, unconscious.

Chapter

12

FRANK AWOKE to the sound of surf filtered through a splitting headache. He rolled over and struggled to his feet. He was on the beach—the lights of the Surf Club about fifty yards away. In the dim moonlight, Frank could make out a blurred trail in the sand leading from the edge of the parking lot where he had been slugged. He had evidently been dragged here, where there would be no casual passersby to spot him.

I feel dizzy, he thought as he trudged back toward the hotel. Who did this to me? He remembered watching Ritt, Auerbach, and Nadia Galinova and wondered whether one of them had attacked him. He checked his watch. It was eleven-thirty.

He entered the Surf Club from the beach entrance in the back and slipped up the back stairs without anyone noticing his sandy, disheveled appearance. He walked down the corridor to his second-floor room, only to remember that he didn't have a key. He knocked on the door. A moment later it opened and Joe was there, staring at him.

"Where've *you* been?" Joe demanded.

"Out on the beach. How was dinner?" Frank stepped inside and sat down on the edge of his bed.

"Great. Chris is fantastic. Just one problem. When we—" Joe stopped when he saw Frank reach for the back of his head and wince.

"Okay, let's have it," he demanded. "What happened, and let's look at that head."

As Joe probed Frank's scalp, Frank gave him a rundown on how he had tried to find out what Auerbach and Ritt had been doing with Galinova.

"The only thing I was able to work out— *ouch!*—watch it back there!—was that Nadia seems really scared of Ritt," he concluded.

"Ritt and Auerbach are up to something, all right," Joe said excitedly. "I saw them together earlier, at the restaurant where I ate with Chris." He filled Frank in on the events of his own evening, including the attempted abduction of Tammy and the receipt for Biodane he had found in Ritt's car.

"Ritt and Auerbach must have driven straight over here after dinner," Joe surmised. "I bet we can crack this case by tomorrow, now that we know about Chuck Herrick—"

"Herrick? What about him?"

"Oh! I forgot to tell you." As he cleaned Frank's wound, Joe told his brother about Herrick. "That kind of makes the Ritts front-runners in Peter Osteen's death," Joe concluded.

Frank frowned. 'Yeah, but they wouldn't be crazy enough to try the same stunt more than once. Especially when people are already suspicious about the last time."

Joe tossed the towel over a chair. "Ritt might figure he can always pull the right strings to make a police problem go away."

Frank stood up and began pacing back and forth. "If Ritt *knows* that this tour is not going to come off, that the whole Hi-Kick promotional scheme will fail, then he'll want to get Junior in with SuperJuice."

Joe considered this. "So he sets up a meeting with Auerbach to make a pitch for Junior. Chris thought it was the other way around. But what do they want with Galinova?"

Frank stopped pacing. "Galinova has a lot of influence on Chris and Tammy. So Ritt tells Auerbach to lean on her to persuade the girls to commit to SuperJuice. One question—"

"What can Ritt use to pressure Nadia?" Joe finished.

They thought about that one for a while, but came up with nothing. "It's late," Frank admitted with a yawn. "Tomorrow we'll tackle the

Nadia question—and we'll visit that gardening store where Ritt bought the Biodane.''

"You think there's any chance of looking at the film of Chaplin's that the police impounded?" Joe wondered, unbuttoning his shirt.

Frank yawned again, and headed for the shower. "We could try, I guess. That is, if we can drag ourselves out of bed tomorrow. Some vacation," he remarked.

The next morning Frank went right to Prindle's office. Prindle greeted them eagerly and asked to hear any news.

The Hardys ran through the events of the previous day, and Prindle groaned when Joe mentioned calling the police the night before.

"I know you had to do it, but if any more of this stuff gets leaked to the press, I'm done for," he said gloomily.

"Any new clippings today?"

"Just a few small pieces on the cable accident yesterday. But that's been played down as an accident because of my own efforts." He made a wry face. "There is a feature on Peter's death coming out in one of the major tabloids next week, though."

Suddenly Joe's eyes widened. "Oh, wow!" he said. "Frank, we forgot to tell him about Auerbach!"

"Auerbach? Something else about Auerbach?" Prindle asked, getting nervous all over again.

Frank turned to Prindle. "We tried to tell you

at the tournament yesterday, but you didn't have time. We found Auerbach in your office yesterday, going through the papers on your desk."

Prindle's eyes got large and round. "He *what?* My *desk?*"

Frank nodded. "We think he was copying down the addresses and phone numbers of some of your players. We told him to hit the road."

Prindle slammed a hand on his desk. "The nerve of that guy! I oughta—if you find him in here again, call the cops! That's exactly the kind of stuff he used to do when he worked for us—"

"He worked for you?" Joe interrupted, shocked.

"Didn't I tell you that? He was with us for three years. He moved over to SuperJuice eighteen months ago, when I got this job instead of him. Officially, he left on good terms, but I know he's been sulking ever since. He'd give anything to see me fail on this project."

"The thing is," Frank said, "he's hanging around with Ritt, and Ritt's starting to look really suspicious. Ken Chaplin told us Ritt may have doctored a player's food last year. Do you think there's anything to that?"

Prindle blinked. "Could be. I wouldn't put a lot past that guy. On the other hand, I don't trust Ken Chaplin either."

"Why not?" Joe asked, even more astonished. "I thought you hired him."

"I did because he was cheap. Chaplin's a good filmmaker, but he has a gambling habit that keeps him in debt. He does a good job, but personally, he's not a guy I'd trust.''

"Does anyone else on the tourney know about our being detectives?'' Frank asked Prindle suddenly.

Prindle pursed his lips. "Nadia Galinova seems to.''

"Nadia?'' Frank frowned. "How?''

"I don't know.'' Prindle seemed perplexed. "She marched in here yesterday evening and chewed my ear off for about half an hour about how we shouldn't let people pry into her private life. I asked her who she meant, and she named you two. She said she had half a mind to resign, but she cares too much about Chris and Tammy. I figured Joe must have told Chris who you guys really are, and Chris told Nadia.''

"No way,'' said Joe, glancing at his brother. "I wanted to tell her, but I figured it would just put her in more danger. So who told Nadia?'' he asked, but got no reply.

The Hardys got up to leave, more confused than when they'd arrived. "If I can help any more, let me know,'' said Prindle, walking them to the door.

"With help like that, we may still be working on this case in ten years,'' Joe muttered to Frank as the office door closed behind them.

"Let's drive out to that garden store you told me about. I want to get something solid on Ritt if we can,'' Frank said.

"Great idea." Joe led the way to their rented car. "That's one guy I wouldn't mind nailing."

It didn't take long to find the Meadowlark Garden Center address. It was located on a major road leading from Laguna Beach to Anaheim. Joe figured the drive would take half an hour, tops.

"After this case is over, we ought to explore the area around here," Frank said as he maneuvered the car out of the lot and onto the highway.

"But then again we might not get a chance to do that," Frank said, when he looked up at the rearview mirror.

"Someone is following us. And after what Prindle told us, I figure these guys play for keeps!"

Chapter

13

THE NAVY BLUE four-by-four truck that had been a few car lengths back was now so close it was practically kissing the rental car's back bumper.

"I guess they want us to know they're following us," Frank said to Joe. "Maybe they're hoping to scare us off. I can't see their faces. Can you?"

Joe turned to peer back, not caring whether the pursuers saw him. "No," he said. "The truck's too high and the windshield's too dark. But if they want to make a statement, maybe we should go ahead and answer them."

Frank glanced over at his brother, a grin flickering across his face. "Are you thinking what I'm thinking?"

Joe nodded solemnly. "My seat belt's fastened. Let 'er fly."

Frank smashed his foot down as hard as he could on the accelerator. The effect was as dramatic as the Hardys intended it to be. The small rental car screamed as it kicked into high gear and peeled out ahead of the lumbering four-wheel-drive truck.

"Did they take the bait?" Frank asked, steering the car onto the Santa Ana Freeway and passing several cars as he moved into the fast lane.

"Yep," Joe said after a moment. "They're coming up fast. That baby definitely is not stock. Someone has done a job on the engine. This rental is no match for it." He laughed. "Looks like you're going to have to do all the work."

"Dad always said that brains can beat muscle any day." Frank gave his brother a quick grin.

As the boys talked, the truck was catching up to them in a series of bull-like rushes, cutting off one driver after another as it changed lanes. Frank, on the other hand, drove smooth and straight.

"You know, if we were on a dirt road, this guy would catch us in a minute," Frank said.

"Then it's a good thing we're on the freeway," Joe said.

"He's still going to catch up to us in a minute if we don't think of something fast," Frank said in reply. Just then a gray-haired man in a glistening black luxury car pulled in front of them, cutting them off. The man was talking on his car phone and clearly hadn't noticed their car.

"Joe, I've got it!" Frank exclaimed as he

slowed to avoid hitting the preoccupied phoner. "And all you have to do is act like your usual crazy self."

The truck was right behind them, one lane to the right to block the Hardys from pulling off quickly at an exit. Frank punched the accelerator after the black luxury car pulled away from them.

As they moved along, the brothers watched not only the pursuing truck, but other cars they were passing. When they overtook a bright yellow van two lanes over, Frank deliberately cut it off, veering into its lane and hitting the brakes. The driver of the van had to hit his brakes, too, to keep from hitting the boys' car. Meanwhile, the Hardys' pursuers shot by them like a rocket.

Just as quickly as he had slowed down, Frank again put the gas to the floor.

Within less than a mile, the boys passed the truck crawling along on their right in the slowest lane. As they went by, the truck accelerated once again.

Very soon the Hardys saw and heard two California Highway Patrol officers on motorcycles enter the highway behind them with lights flashing and sirens screaming. So did the driver of the truck, Joe noted with satisfaction as it finally used all its power to pull away. Within seconds, the police were alongside the brothers' car, waving them off to the shoulder.

When the officer walked up beside Frank's

window, he found, to his surprise, two grinning faces staring up at him.

"Officer, you're never going to believe how glad I am to see you," said Frank.

All Joe could do was laugh.

Frank led Joe into the Meadowlark Garden Center's large greenhouse, where he'd spotted the shop's manager squatting and snipping leaves from some potted plants.

"These grow like weeds in this climate," said the manager, a cheerful older man with a fringe of white hair around a bald, shiny scalp. "May I help you gentlemen?"

"We'd appreciate a little information," Frank replied. "Do you carry something called Biodane?"

"Biodane?" echoed the manager, getting to his feet. "You fellas want to be real careful with Biodane. It's nasty stuff."

"We aren't planning to use it," Joe assured him. "We just want to know what it is."

"It's a heavy-duty pesticide. And I mean *heavy-duty*. Active ingredient is nicotine, and in concentrated form it'd kill off a herd of buffalo. Most folks wouldn't want it around the house, and I think they're perfectly right."

"We were wondering if you had a customer buy some a few days back," Joe said. "Do you remember?"

"Well, yes, as a matter of fact," the manager

said without hesitating. "An impatient fella, I recall."

"What did he look like?" Frank asked, trying to stifle his own impatience.

The manager reflected. "He was kind of husky, middle-aged, with curly reddish blond hair. I warned him how strong it was, and he got kind of angry. Said he just wanted Biodane, not advice." The manager shook his head. "Nasty fella."

Frank and Joe exchanged a quick look. The man had given them a fine thumbnail description of George Ritt, Sr.

"Nicotine," Frank said as the brothers got back in their car. "Colorless and tasteless. And about as toxic as poison gets."

"Okay. Ritt had the means to kill Osteen," Joe said. "And he had motivation—maybe. But what about opportunity? And, anyway, you don't think Ritt put Biodane in the Hi-Kick, do you? All the players drank it, and the other three didn't get sick."

"Right," answered Frank. "But I don't think Ritt bought it for his rose garden, either."

The brothers rode in silence for a while, pondering all the pieces of the puzzle. "Well, we always suspected George Ritt," Joe said finally. "Now we have one more reason to suspect him. But what about Auerbach? And Galinova? What does she know about us, and how did she find out?"

"Maybe she doesn't really know anything. She might just have wanted us fired. She sure doesn't like the idea of you distracting Chris from volleyball."

"Yeah, but she talked about our snooping," Joe reminded him. "She could have just told Prindle we were bothering Chris and Tammy."

"But then Prindle might not have backed her up," Frank suggested. "This story is just her word against ours. And she knows she carries a lot of weight within the sport."

"The weird thing about this—if you take the different elements—" Joe said, "the anonymous letters, the phone calls, the attempted kidnapping, the exploding volleyball, the poison, and that truck that tried to run us down, they all seem as if they must have been done by different people. It's hard to put all those things on any one suspect. On the other hand, it's even harder to imagine a lot of people working together to destroy Hi-Kick's investment."

"Yeah, I know what you mean," Frank said. "But if, for instance, Galinova is in on this, she's not alone. She'd have to be working with someone else. Maybe Ritt, maybe Auerbach."

"So now what?" Joe asked with a sigh.

"Now we drop in on Detective O'Boyle and see if the tox screen turned up anything interesting. And maybe we can ask to see Ken Chaplin's confiscated film."

"Sounds good," Joe said. "Then we can get

lunch and maybe watch a little volleyball. What time—"

Whap!

A sharp explosive sound cut Joe off in midsentence, and acrid smoke drifted into the car.

"What was that?" demanded Joe.

"I don't know," replied Frank.

"Great. What'd our horoscope say today? 'Avoid all transportation, especially rental cars'?" He waited. "Well, what's up?"

They were riding at just under the forty-five-mile-per-hour speed limit, but a yellow sign up ahead warned of unusually sharp curves. Frank turned the steering wheel.

The car failed to respond.

"That 'bang' left us without any steering!" Frank shouted.

He hit the brake pedal. The car started to slow, but then, to Frank's horror, the pedal suddenly gave way and sank to the floor.

"Uh-oh," said Joe. "I don't think I want to know any more."

"You have to!" Frank shouted. "It took the brakes, too! Brace yourself!"

The road curved to the left. Straight ahead, a clump of tall palms loomed.

"We're going to hit them!" Frank yelled. "Hold on, Joe!"

Chapter

14

"CAN WE JUMP?" yelled Joe.

"Nope. Too fast!" Frank shouted, downshifting before he yanked the handle of the emergency brake. The forward motion still sent the car lurching off the road, the right front bumper slamming into the trunk of a palm. Sliding sideways and raising a huge cloud of dust, the rear swung around and smashed into another palm. The car was wedged in solidly.

Frank felt as though his seat belt had nearly cut him in half. He looked across at Joe. His brother's eyes were shut.

"Joe? Can you hear me? Are you hurt? *Joe!*"

Joe grunted, his eyes still closed. "My shoulder feels like someone hit it with a sledgehammer," he mumbled finally. "Otherwise, I feel great."

Frank opened his door, and they struggled out on his side, since Joe's door was jammed. "Not that it makes much difference at this point, but let's find out what caused this," Frank said, checking to make sure none of his bones was broken before moving to the front of the car.

"Score two for seat belts," Joe muttered as he joined his brother.

Frank managed to pop the hood of the wrecked car, and he and Joe peered into the battered interior. "Just what I thought," Frank said, noting the grease splattered all over the left side of the engine and scratches on the inside of the fender from flying bits of metal. "Someone put a small explosive on the steering box. The brake lines must have been cut by one of the exploding pieces of metal." He slammed the hood down in disgust.

"Who?" Joe asked, voicing what was in both their minds. "The guy who chased us in the truck?"

Frank shrugged. "All I know is, I'm checking out every vehicle belonging to everyone connected with the tournament. Anyone who turns up with a customized truck had better watch out for me."

"Yeah," agreed Joe. "And while we're at it, we might as well look around for any explosives experts, too."

Just then a battered, dusty station wagon pulled up by the side of the road, and two long-haired, shirtless surfers, their boards on a rack on top of the car, stared at the scene.

"You dudes all right?" called the driver.

"We're fine," called Joe. "But the car—"

"The car is a total wipeout," said the driver's friend. "Strictly scrap metal."

"We need to get to Laguna Beach," Frank said.

"No sweat," replied the driver. "Hop in back. You sure you're all in one piece?"

"Almost," Joe replied, sliding into the wagon and flexing his arm.

Half an hour later Frank and Joe were in Laguna Beach police headquarters, sitting in Dan O'Boyle's cramped cubicle of an office. O'Boyle had arranged for a tow truck to pick up the rental car, and now he was studying the brothers.

"This isn't a big city," O'Boyle said philosophically, "and I'm an easygoing kind of guy. Some people might even think of me as a dumb hick cop. You don't, though, do you?"

"No, sir," Frank said dully.

"Good. Because since I first saw you two at that tournament on the beach, we've had an unexpected death, an attempted abduction, and now a mysterious and very nasty road accident. These are the things I *know* about you." He paused. "I think it's time for some straight talk."

"Actually," said Joe, "believe it or not, we

were on our way here when our car got wrecked. To have that straight talk.''

O'Boyle pulled out a pad of lined, yellow paper and a pen. "Let's hear it," he said briefly.

"Our father is Fenton Hardy," said Frank, "a private investigator back East. We work on cases, too, sometimes. We happened to be around when weird stuff started happening at the tournament, and Mr. Prindle asked us to investigate.''

"Investigate what?" asked the detective.

Frank and Joe quickly described the anonymous letters, the phone calls, the exploding volleyball, and the truck that had chased them that morning. The detective already knew about the other incidents.

When the Hardys had finished, O'Boyle said nothing—he only stared. Finally he spoke up, "Aren't you boys a little young for this kind of thing? Meaning no offense, of course."

"We can handle it," Joe said tersely. "If you want confirmation, you can call our dad."

O'Boyle stood up. "I think I have to do just that," he said. "In some other office, where I can have a little privacy. You boys wait here."

When O'Boyle returned ten minutes later, his pained expression had been replaced with an amused grin. "Well, now," he boomed as he sat down at his desk. "I thought I'd heard the name Fenton Hardy before, and it turns out we have some common friends in the law enforcement business. So you were coming in to see me, anyway, were you? What was it you wanted to ask?"

"We were wondering about the tox screen you're doing on Peter Osteen," Frank said. "Are the results in yet?"

"We expect them in this afternoon," the detective replied. "What else?"

"Have you looked at the film you confiscated from Ken Chaplin yet?" Joe spoke up. "Did anything in it seem out of line?"

"We've run that film half a dozen times," O'Boyle said with a sigh. "It's got pretty shots of the beach, a bunch of volleyball action sequences, and some folks drinking that Hi-Kick gunk and smacking their lips. Not a thing you could use, though. You're welcome to look yourselves."

"That would be great," said Frank.

"I'll have it set up for you." O'Boyle reached for his phone. "One thing, though," he said before he dialed. "No more hush-hush stuff, okay? We share what we know from now on."

"Yes, sir," Joe replied.

O'Boyle led them to a room with a projector and screen, then left the Hardys alone to watch the film.

Joe sat back and watched the series of shots, all of them exactly as O'Boyle had described. Halfway through, the film switched to shots of the tournament's first match—mostly of players drinking cups of Hi-Kick between plays.

As Joe watched a shot of Peter Osteen, he

wondered again if the poison had been in that cup. But if so, how did it get there without hurting the others? Joe peered intently at the screen as the scene changed to one of the cheering crowd. There had to be something there they could use.

Suddenly Frank reached over and pressed the Pause button. "Wait a minute," he said. "Look at that."

Joe studied the still shot of the front row of the bleachers, where the Ritts were sitting, deep in conversation. Frank ran the film in slow motion, and Joe watched as Junior spoke to his father. Junior seemed nervous and was pointing at the court. In response the older Ritt swung his head around and said something short and angry. Junior shut his mouth and looked even more unhappy.

"Junior's worried," said Frank.

"Yeah, and his dad told him to keep his mouth shut," Joe agreed.

A shot of the players between serves showed all four of them breathing hard and sweating.

The final sequence showed Peter Osteen pitching forward onto the sand.

"No shot of Ritt pouring Biodane into the cooler," Joe said. "Too bad."

Frank stood up. "Let's see about getting another car. We need to talk to Prindle."

It was midafternoon when the Hardys reached the Surf Club's parking lot and knocked on Prindle's door. There was no answer, but as they turned to leave they saw Ken Chaplin drive up and head for the film crew trailer.

"Mr. Chaplin!" called Frank.

"Can't talk now, Frank," called Chaplin. "Got to hurry back. We're between matches."

After he punched in the security code on the alarm system, unlocked the front door, and opened it, Frank and Joe peered inside. It looked as though every inch of the limited space was filled with equipment, plastic containers of chemicals, and boxes.

"Have you seen Mr. Prindle?" Joe called into the trailer.

"If he's not in the men's locker room," Chaplin answered, "he's at the court."

The Hardys found Prindle in the locker room, where most of the players had gathered until it was time to take their places on the court or in the bleachers for the next match.

"What's up?" Prindle asked as he joined the Hardys in the empty gym for a little privacy.

"Plenty." Joe filled Prindle in on all that had happened so far that day.

"Listen," he said when Joe had finished, "You sure you guys are all right? I don't want to be responsible for your getting hurt or anything—"

"Too late now," Frank quipped. "Actually, what we need from you is information. Do you know anyone connected with the tournament who owns a truck like the one that chased us?"

"No," Prindle replied. "And it sounds like a truck I'd remember. Of course, I don't notice what everyone who works here drives." He paused. "Anything else?"

"Yeah," said Joe. "I was wondering, the day Peter died, did the players seem more burned out than usual? It was hard for us to tell, but you've seen a lot of these games up close."

"Maybe." Prindle looked perplexed. Then he checked his watch. "Listen, the match is going to start soon. I've got to get back to work. Why don't you talk to the players about how they felt?"

"Good idea," said Frank as Prindle hurried off. "Why don't you do that, Joe? I'm going back to the room."

"How come?"

"I want to call O'Boyle to find out if those test results came in. I'll meet you in the room in, say, half an hour."

Joe returned to the locker room, and was relieved to see that Junior had wandered off. The other players were laughing and joking in small groups. Brad Conlin was stretched out on a bench, talking with Mark Donahue. They looked up when Joe entered and waved him over.

"Aren't you working today?" Brad asked. "Just twenty minutes till match time."

"Uh, right." Joe was taken off guard. He'd been so involved in the case that he'd almost forgotten he was supposed to be a working volunteer. "Prindle gave us the day off," he improvised. "I guess he figured some other guys ought to get a chance to field volleyballs on national TV."

The players laughed, and Joe sat down on the bench next to Conlin. "I'll be in the bleachers, though," Joe added. "It's Junior and Buzz Maestren against Scooter Lenz and his new partner, right?"

The players nodded. Pretending to make small talk, Joe then asked, "How are you two feeling, anyway?"

"How are we feeling," Donahue echoed, mystified. "Fine. Why?"

"No reason," Joe hedged. "You looked so beat after that match the other day. But I guess that's normal after something like that, huh?"

"I wouldn't say normal, exactly," Donahue replied. "I mean, I felt bad all that day. So did you, right, Conlin? A bug must have been going around. That's why we didn't react right away when Peter started slowing down."

"Yeah," Conlin remembered. "At first he looked like the rest of us felt."

Just then one of the other players checked his watch and called out, "It's time!" There was a general hubbub in the locker room as the players got ready to hit the bleachers.

"Coming, Joe?" Donahue asked as he and Conlin headed for the door.

"Go ahead." Joe waved them on. "I'm supposed to meet Frank at our room. We'll see you at the match."

By the time Joe was finishing his conversation with Conlin and Donahue, Frank had arrived at their room.

As he punched in the first few digits of O'Boyle's phone number, Frank had the feeling that something had moved across the room. Instantly alert, he spun around—and saw that the closet door was open.

Out of the closet sprang Nadia Galinova, eyes fixed and staring. In her upraised hand was a long, gleaming knife!

Chapter

15

FRANK HIT THE FLOOR as Galinova's razor-sharp blade buried itself in the bedding where he'd been sitting a moment before. Instantly he scrambled to his feet and backed away from the knife, which she had retrieved.

Nadia slowly advanced toward him, holding the weapon waist high. The limited space gave Frank little room to maneuver.

"Nadia, you're making a big mistake. I don't mean you any harm."

Nadia paid no attention and continued to advance. Frank took one more step back—and found himself up against a wall. Realizing he was trapped, he searched for a weapon—any kind of weapon. Just then Galinova made her move and threw herself at him with the knife in her outstretched hand.

"No, you don't!" Frank pivoted and grabbed her knife hand. Pulling her off balance, he chopped down on her wrist with the edge of his hand. Nadia's weapon fell to the floor. Frank stooped quickly to retrieve it as Nadia crumpled to the floor in a heap.

"Nadia?" called Frank.

She made no response.

"Nadia?" Frank knelt down on the floor beside her just as the room door opened and Joe rushed in.

"Frank, Conlin and Donahue said—"

He stopped as he rounded the corner of the bed.

"What happened here?"

Frank explained. Astounded, Joe stared at the hunched figure. "Nadia?" he said softly. "Tell us why."

"You can talk to us or to the police," Frank pointed out. "It's your choice."

She raised her head and, with Frank's help, got up and sat on the edge of the bed. Her face was pale.

"I didn't want to hurt you," she said to Frank, her eyes lowered. "I meant to scare you, that's all. Not that it makes a difference now." Her voice sounded thick and mechanical.

"But why scare him?" Joe demanded.

"Because you were about to ruin my life!" she cried, and then forced herself to settle down again.

Joe sighed and sat down on the other bed,

facing her. "Nadia," he said, trying to be patient, "I think you'd better tell us the whole story."

Slowly and with difficulty, Nadia began to talk. She began by telling the Hardys how she had defected to America eighteen years earlier, leaving her family behind. Her defection caused her family to be badly treated by the government.

Five years ago, Galinova explained, she had learned that her younger sister, Hana, was seriously ill. There was then no treatment available for her in Eastern Europe. If Hana remained there, she would die. Only with medical help in the West might she survive.

But there was no way to bring Hana to this country. Nevertheless, Nadia had gone to powerful people and told them her problem. Hana had been smuggled out of the country, and she illegally entered the United States, where her life had been saved.

"So what's the problem?" Joe asked, perplexed.

Galinova eyed him coolly.

Somehow, she told the brothers, George Ritt had discovered Hana's illegal status. He had threatened Nadia with having Hana arrested and either put in jail or deported unless Nadia did as Ritt demanded.

"Which was?" prompted Frank.

"He and a man who works for another drink company—"

"Auerbach," said Joe.

"Yes. They want me to get Chris and Tammy to sign a contract with this SuperJuice. Then Mr. Ritt's son will also sign a contract, and the others will follow. I tried to do this, but Chris and Tammy said they would not."

"But what does that have to do with us?" Frank asked. "Why'd you go after me?"

"Because Ritt told me who you are," she said. "Detectives for the INS—the Immigration and Naturalization Service. He told me you want to find Hana and take her away." She was fighting tears now. "This I cannot allow."

Frank and Joe stared at her, astonished. "And you believed him?" Frank asked.

"Of course I did," she said with a small shrug. "This is not something to joke about."

"Nadia," Joe said urgently, "listen to me. Ritt lied to you. We're not from the INS. We have no interest in your sister. Ritt and Auerbach have treated you very badly. But if you'll trust us, we'll see that they pay for what they've done."

Galinova seemed almost hopeful now. "How?"

"We can't say right now," Frank answered. "But no harm will come to Hana—or to you. For the time being, don't let them know that we've had this talk. Pretend things are just as they were between you."

Then they persuaded Galinova to leave without telling her any more. After she had gone, Frank turned to Joe. He was steaming.

"Let's make sure Ritt and Auerbach get what they deserve. They've fooled around with too many people's lives."

"The best way to get Ritt is to nail him for murder," Joe pointed out. "Did you get the results from the tox screen yet?"

"No, I was interrupted," Frank said wryly, picking up the receiver that he'd dropped by the bed. "I'll do it now."

"Not a trace of nicotine in Osteen's body," he told Joe after he'd hung up.

"Then Ritt didn't poison him." Joe sounded almost disappointed.

"Not with Biodane." He thought for a moment. Then he said, "Time for the tournament. Let's go root against Junior."

The match between the Ritt-Maestren team and that of Lenz and his new partner, Whitey Mullins of Redondo Beach, was tied at two–two when Joe and Frank squeezed into the front-row section.

Richard Prindle paced nervously along the side of the court directly in front of the boys. When he noticed Frank and Joe, he went up to them.

"How's the match going?" Frank asked.

"Junior's off his game, and he's losing his cool. He keeps trying jump serves, and they keep hitting the net or landing way out of bounds."

Frank glanced over Prindle's shoulder in time

to watch Buzz Maestren serve to Whitey Mullins, who bumped the ball to Scooter Lenz. Junior came forward, assuming Lenz would set for Mullins to spike. Instead, Scooter leapt up and slammed the ball down just behind Junior. "Side out," Frank murmured along with the announcer. He watched as Junior whirled around to face his partner.

"Where were you?" Junior screamed. "I can't play this game by myself."

His display of temper drew scattered catcalls. Frank noticed that several tournament players were delighting in booing Junior. Mark Donahue leaned toward Frank and muttered, "Want to bet Junior is going to need a new partner next week?"

Joe overheard him and laughed. Frank faced front again and noticed for the first time that George Ritt, Sr., was seated in the third row of the bleachers directly across the court. He was watching his son with a stern, rigid expression. Beside him sat Todd Auerbach, whose expression was equally grim.

The audience roared as a perfect jump serve by Scooter Lenz gave his team the lead. No question who most of this crowd was rooting for, Frank noted.

The ball was back in play. Junior jumped to spike the ball. Whitey Mullins leapt with his hands high to block it. The ball hung frozen between their hands, then dropped to the sand on Junior's side of the net.

"Ten—eight," the loudspeakers echoed. Frank watched as Junior kicked the ball savagely. The audience responded with louder boos. The referee leaned toward the surly player, apparently giving him a warning. Frank glanced across the court to see that George senior had risen to his feet. Auerbach was trying to pull him back down.

Junior had lost his poise, and five minutes later his team had lost the match, the score three games to two. Head down, he stomped off the court, not stopping to shake hands with the winners.

Buzz Maestren gave George senior an icy look. "Find another sucker!" the Hardys heard him shout. "I've had it!"

"Look, there are Chris and Tammy," Joe said to Frank, pointing at them in the crowd filing out across the court. "Be right back." He sprinted across to the girls, dodging through the milling fans like a broken-field runner.

Frank remained in his seat, watching Ken Chaplin and his crew set up for an interview with the winning team.

He watched Vern's expert maneuverings with the camera while Ken did the interviewing. It must take years to become a really good technician, he reflected.

Then he got an idea. He blinked, concentrating hard.

A moment later Joe was back in his seat, reporting breathlessly to Frank, "Chris and

Tammy want to make dinner for us at their place tonight. I told them we'd be there at seven o'clock.''

"Fine," Frank said absently, still watching the interview. "Listen, did you talk to the players about being tired the other day?"

"Oh, yeah," Joe said. "I forgot to tell you. They said they felt out of it all through the match. That's why they didn't react to Osteen's staggering around right away. They all felt pretty much that way." He glanced at his brother. "What do you think it means?"

"Tell you later. Right now, how do you like the idea of confronting the Ritts?"

Joe's eyes lit up, and his fists involuntarily clenched. "I *like* it. When?"

"First, I want to have a look around Chaplin's trailer. I've got an idea about that, too, and it looks like the crew's going to be tied up here for a while. Then we go after George junior and senior."

Frank spotted Prindle and called his name. When Prindle came over, Frank asked him for the Ritts' address. Prindle wasn't eager to give it to him, but he finally did relent. As soon as Frank had pocketed the slip of paper with the address, he took off.

"What's the hurry?" Joe asked.

"I want to be out of Chaplin's trailer before Chaplin shows up."

Joe slowed down a little. "I see your point."

It was a simple matter to get past the trailer's newly installed security system, since Frank had made a note of the letters Vern had punched to silence the alarm. "Real hard to remember," he commented as he punched in the code. " 'Vern.' Nobody'd think of trying that."

Joe was the expert at lock-picking, and Frank stood back as he worked the padlock.

Five minutes later the boys were inside. Joe closed the door, and Frank switched on the light. He looked around at the piles of technical gear and shelves lined with huge plastic bottles labeled "Toner," "Acetone," and "Distilled Water."

Quickly and efficiently, he began his search. It didn't take long. Fifteen minutes later he straightened up and said, "Okay. Let's go."

"Great." Joe headed for the door. "But are you going to tell me what you were looking for?"

"Sure, but not now. First I want to talk to the Ritts."

"Wonderful," Joe said as they left the trailer, being careful to lock it and reset the alarm. "My own brother's playing guessing games with me."

The address Prindle had given the Hardys was that of a house George Ritt owned in Laguna Hills. Despite their mission, Frank found himself distracted again by the spectacular views as their new rented car wound up among the rocky heights.

Frank drove on past the large, two-story, white-columned house and down the road about twenty yards farther. He parked on the shoulder, and got out.

"Why'd you park here?" Joe asked, walking back toward the house beside his brother.

Frank smiled enigmatically. "I want to take them by surprise."

As they approached the massive front doors of the impressive mansion, Frank and Joe could hear the muffled sounds of angry voices inside.

"Doesn't sound like a happy family," Joe remarked as the brothers mounted the front steps.

"Surprise, surprise," said Frank. He started to ring the doorbell.

At the sound of the chimes, the yelling stopped abruptly. The door swung open and Junior stood there, red-faced and scowling.

"What do *you* want?"

"We need to talk," said Frank.

"We've got nothing to say to you."

"Okay, then, just listen."

Junior muttered something and stepped back to let the brothers in.

He led them to a large living room where Ritt, Sr., was sitting. He jumped up, startled and annoyed.

"You've got some nerve, waltzing in here. Beat it, or I'll call the cops!" he said.

"Go ahead." Frank gestured to a phone on a

nearby table. "Then we can have a nice conversation about gardening supplies."

Junior's eyes widened. "Dad—" he said in a surprisingly small voice.

"Shut your mouth!" growled his father. He turned to Frank. "I don't know what you mean."

"We mean Biodane," said Frank. "A toxic pesticide, which we can prove you bought recently. To kill bugs in the roses, was it? Or moles in the potato patch?"

Ritt flashed him a cruel, hard grin.

"You wise guys have been snooping around, haven't you. Not smart. You picked the wrong man to mess with."

He strolled over to a fancy cabinet and opened a drawer. He pulled out a large, blue-steel automatic pistol, which he pointed straight at Joe. To both Hardys, the barrel looked as big as the mouth of a tunnel.

"See? Biodane isn't the only way to get rid of annoying pests," said Ritt.

He cocked the automatic with a loud, metallic click.

Chapter

16

"DAD!" JUNIOR SQUAWKED. "What are you—"

"Keep quiet, boy!" Ritt kept his eyes and the gun fixed on the Hardys. "These squirts can put us both in prison, don't you see that? No one is going to do that to George Ritt—or his son."

"There's something you should understand," said Frank. "About Peter Osteen—"

"We didn't want him to die!" Junior cried out.

"I told you to shut up!" his father snarled. "Don't turn gutless on me, son."

"It wasn't Biodane that killed Osteen," Joe said. "If that's what you're scared about, you can relax." He couldn't take his eyes off the gun muzzle that was now aimed at his stomach.

"What do you mean?" asked Junior. "Dad, did you hear what he said?"

130

"It's a trick, son, that's all. They'll say anything to save their necks. But it's too late."

Frank said, "We just learned the results of a tox screen the police ordered. There was no nicotine in Osteen's body. That means no Biodane. Scooter Lenz says Peter didn't eat any fruit before the match. That's how you tried to get him, right? You made a weak solution of Biodane that you figured would make him sick. Then you injected it into the fruit. When he died, you thought you'd miscalculated."

"What we're going to do," said Ritt, ignoring him completely, "is take a little drive to a nice, out-of-the-way canyon I know of, where your bodies won't be found for days, maybe weeks—"

"Dad! He says we didn't kill Peter!"

"If he murders us," Joe said to Junior, "you're an accessory. Is that what you want?"

Junior, stupefied, opened his mouth, then closed it again. Then he shook his head.

"Shut up, you," Ritt, Sr., roared at Joe, "or I'll finish you right here and now. Son, do what I say. Don't I always do what's best for you?"

"What's *best* for me?" said Junior, astounded. "Sure, right, what's *best* for me! Like wasting my life trying to make me into a champion athlete, when I don't *want* to be one! Now you want to make me a murderer, too. Well, sorry, Dad. I *won't* be!"

Junior lunged forward and grabbed his father's gun arm. Before Frank or Joe could go for the weapon, it went off with an earsplitting report that echoed through the room.

In the shocked silence that followed, Joe was able to snatch the gun out of the older man's hand. He held it on both the Ritts while Frank moved to the telephone and called the police.

"What's *best* for me," Frank heard Junior mutter to his father as he hung up the phone. Frank looked again at the two of them, and was surprised at the extreme hate in the son's eyes and the uncertainty and fear in the father's.

"One thing I want to know before the police arrive," Frank said crisply. "Why did you try to force Nadia to go after us?"

"Auerbach told me you were professional snoops," the elder Ritt snarled. "He wanted you gone."

"How'd *he* know who we were?" Joe asked.

Ritt shrugged. "He didn't say."

Sirens sounded in the distance. Detective O'Boyle and his partner, Ericsson, entered the mansion. O'Boyle took in the situation quickly and turned to the Hardys.

"All right. Let's have it."

Frank told him everything that had happened—except for Auerbach's part and the attack by Galinova. Nadia would be terrified if she thought the police knew about her.

"Why didn't you call me before you came up here?" O'Boyle demanded sternly.

Frank shook his head. "Maybe we were wrong. I didn't expect Ritt to go for a gun."

"It was *his* idea," said Junior, his face red with fear and anger. "All his doing."

"Son!" exclaimed Ritt, obviously hurt.

"That Biodane stuff—the rest of it is hidden in the basement."

"You're willing to testify against your father?" asked Ericsson.

"Yes, sir." Junior met Ericsson's gaze. "I'm no murderer. He belongs in jail."

As Ericsson handcuffed the two Ritts and herded them out to the police car, O'Boyle paused to say goodbye to the Hardys. "Call me if you find anything. And watch out for yourselves. If you got killed around here it would be a definite black mark on my record."

The brothers smiled wanly, and O'Boyle followed the others out.

As Frank and Joe returned to their car, Joe said, "That felt good, but why do I get the feeling we were only dealing with small fry here?"

Frank nodded. "The way I see it, George Ritt thought he was masterminding a plot to eliminate the competition for his son. But what was really happening was that Auerbach was manipulating him to help destroy Frosty's reputation."

"Right." Joe climbed into the passenger seat. "Auerbach wanted revenge for getting passed over at Frosty."

"And to make his reputation at SuperJuice by stealing the world's best players," Frank added.

"Yeah. Ritt was his most powerful tool for doing that. But he probably had others."

"Bingo." Frank started the car's engine. "See if you can guess who."

It took about two seconds for Joe to come up with the name. "Ken Chaplin, isn't it?" he demanded.

Frank nodded. "And I think his assistant, Vern, must be in on it, too."

"Shouldn't we tell the police?" Joe wanted to know.

"We don't have any proof, but later I think we might be able to come up with it."

"So what do you figure? Junior chased us down the highway in the four-by-four? With his money he'd have access to any truck he wanted," Joe said.

"The anonymous notes and phone calls we can chalk up to Auerbach's warming up while he figured out how to wreck the tournament. But then there were all those complicated bits of action."

"Right," said Joe. "Like the exploding volleyball."

"And the bomb in our car. And the wire cable pulling the anchor loose at just the right time. I was watching Chaplin and Vern film an interview when it hit me—all those pranks were like movie special effects. And when we searched their trailer, I found everything they'd need to coat exploding volleyballs and install timed explosives."

"I guess they complained about their own equipment being vandalized to throw people off the track."

"And to give them an excuse to add a security system to their trailer. It was really installed to keep people from finding their bomb-making equipment."

"Do you think they attacked Tammy?" Joe asked him.

Frank looked grim. "I don't know yet. But if they did, not only are they more dangerous than I thought, but you and I owe them one."

"I still think we should just turn them all over to the cops," Joe said when he and Frank were dressing to go to dinner at Tammy's house. "Why let them run loose?"

"I don't want them spilling the beans about Nadia's situation with her sister, just yet," Frank reminded him. "It'd be the first thing Auerbach would do, just to make them suffer, too."

"Frank, Nadia tried to stab you, remember?"

Frank bent to tie his shoes. "She was lied to and put under a lot of pressure," he insisted. "She'll have to confess the whole story about her sister eventually. But maybe they'll go easier on her if she helps bring in Auerbach."

"So that's your plan. But what if Ritt tells about Auerbach?"

"I think Mr. George Ritt, Sr., is afraid of Auerbach, and Junior may not know," Frank answered.

"So let me get this straight—you're going to talk Nadia into reporting Auerbach personally?"

"Why not? Then she can testify against him and Ritt. She didn't do anything really wrong concerning her sister, anyway. They'll probably give her a break."

"You think she'll trust us enough to contact the police if we tell her to?"

Frank shrugged. "It's worth a try. I'll call her tonight, after we get back from dinner and before we go back to the film trailer for our proof. That way," he added with a mischievous gleam in his eye, "I'll be able to tell her the girls are safe and at home, too."

Frank started to steer the car out of the hotel parking lot when he glanced in his rearview mirror. What he saw made his hands turn to ice on the steering wheel.

"Uh-oh," Frank said in a low voice.

"What?" Joe said. "Did you forget your—"

Joe's words froze in his throat. As he'd turned toward Frank, a movement in the backseat had caught his eye. He turned to see two figures kneeling on the floor behind them. One had a sawed-off shotgun pressed into the nape of Frank's neck.

"Look straight ahead and keep quiet," said the man holding the gun.

Joe felt something cold and metallic against his own neck.

"Remember, we can kill you both in an instant, so behave."

It was the voice of Ken Chaplin.

Chapter

17

"WELL, WELL," said Frank, eyeing the two men in the mirror. "You *are* in this, too, Vern. I wasn't sure."

"Zip your lip and drive," ordered Chaplin. "Turn left here."

"I guess they *did* try to kidnap Tammy," Joe said to his brother, facing front. "We were wondering about that," he added to their captors.

"We just wanted to scare her." Vern was being drawn into the conversation, as the Hardys had intended. "She wouldn't cooperate, though. That was a problem. That girl has a mean kick."

"Shut up, Vern." Chaplin nudged the shotgun a little deeper into Frank's neck. But Chaplin couldn't seem to resist taunting the Hardys himself.

"We've been onto you for a while now," he bragged. "Ever since you seemed so interested in that volleyball we rigged for Chris. I don't know what kind of snoops you are, but you sure aren't professionals. We saw you coming out of our trailer this afternoon from fifty yards away."

"It was unbelievable," Vern crowed. "There we were, lugging all our equipment back when we looked up and saw you guys locking our door."

They were driving north, with the sun low over the horizon on their left. Traffic was light, and Joe had little hope that the occupants of other cars would see the guns and notify the police.

"Why did you do it?" he heard Frank ask. "Just for money?"

Chaplin laughed derisively. " 'Just for money?' " he mimicked. "You make it sound like nothing. Try living without it for years. You'll come to realize it's the only thing that's important. Vern here has always known that, but I had to learn."

"Yep." Vern cackled, making the cold barrel of his gun tickle the back of Joe's neck. "We may not like that George Ritt much, but he pays well. And Auerbach—he's got brains."

"Slow down," Chaplin said abruptly. "You'll see a driveway on the left. Turn into it, and drive toward the water."

The driveway led past a series of old parking lots occasionally used by beach visitors during the day. The pavement was cracked and full of potholes. Grass and weeds sprung up out of the asphalt of the parking lots.

In the lot nearest the beach, a single car was waiting. Joe eyed it apprehensively. It was a red sports car—like the one he'd seen Auerbach drive. Joe could see someone in the driver's seat as Chaplin ordered Frank to pull up next to the car.

"Turn off the engine," Chaplin ordered next. "Leave the key in the ignition."

Frank did as he was told. Joe peered toward the ocean, squinting into the sun, which hung just at the horizon. He made out a small building at the edge of the water. It was faded and weather-beaten—clearly long unused. Behind the building a run-down pier jutted into the Pacific. Some of its pilings tilted at odd angles, and much of the planking was broken.

Vern got out and covered Frank and Joe with his sawed-off shotgun.

"Out," he said. "Take it real easy."

As the Hardys got out of their car, Todd Auerbach got out of the other one with a canvas athletic bag.

Joe stared at the man who had masterminded so much trouble. Auerbach was calm and looked as if he were going for a swim instead of planning to murder two teenagers. He greeted the Hardys. "Let's walk."

139

The beach was deserted as they walked toward the old pier. Auerbach led the way. Chaplin and Vern, guns in hand, brought up the rear.

"So is SuperJuice worth it?" Joe couldn't resist asking as they crossed the sand.

Auerbach gave a sharp bark of laughter. "SuperJuice is worth nothing," he replied. "I, on the other hand, am worth more every day because of my brilliant coup over Hi-Kick soda."

"You won't get away with it," Frank informed him. "You know Ritt's already under arrest. He'll eventually tell the police about you if it will lighten his sentence."

"He'll have to," Joe added. "They're going to charge him with murder."

"He'll get off," Auerbach said smoothly.

"How do you figure that?" Frank asked.

"Because he didn't commit murder," Auerbach replied, amused. "If anyone did, it was me."

Joe took a quick step toward Auerbach before Vern's shotgun was jammed against his lower back, reminding him to stay back. "What do you mean?" he said then in a low, carefully controlled voice.

"Simple." Auerbach seemed to be enjoying himself. "I was snooping around in the locker room before the match, checking to make sure Ritt hadn't bungled things again and forgotten to put the Biodane in the fruit, and I saw that

140

Osteen hadn't eaten any of it. I put two and two together and figured he was holding back because of Hi-Kick's high sugar content."

"So?" Joe prodded.

"So I switched the contents of the cooler," Auerbach bragged. "I convinced a ballboy that a cooler full of SuperJuice, which contains no sugar, would be much better for the athletes than that gooey stuff Prindle makes them drink."

Joe's step faltered as Auerbach stepped out onto the pier and he and Frank were herded after him. Osteen really had died of hypoglycemic shock! But it was deliberately induced—not an accident!

"Fortunately, I'll never be caught for that one," Auerbach continued. "I've given Ken and Vern here very large bankrolls and two one-way tickets to faraway places. You boys will soon be out of the way. Ritt has no idea how Osteen really died. And I'll eventually take over SuperJuice myself, just for the fun of running Frosty out of business."

"Vern, Ken," Joe heard Frank say sharply. "You haven't done anything too serious yet. If you kill us, it's Murder One. Nowhere you can go is far enough to hide from a charge like that."

Vern handed his shotgun to Auerbach, went to Frank, and threw a roundhouse right to his jaw. Frank dropped to his knees. Joe moved toward his brother but stopped as two guns swung toward his head. Frank struggled to his feet.

"I've been wanting to do that," growled Vern, taking the shotgun back from Auerbach. "Keep mouthing off and I'll do it again."

Auerbach unzipped his canvas bag and took out two coiled lengths of rope. He gave them to Vern.

"You have to get wet," he said to the boys. "But it *is* summer."

Chaplin and Elliott forced the brothers at gun-point into the water, next to the pilings of the old pier.

"This is far enough, I think," Chaplin said.

The water was two feet deep. Vern walked to a piling and gestured to Joe with his gun barrel. "Get over here," he ordered.

When Joe did so, Vern said, "Sit."

Joe hesitated, but Vern cocked the hammer on his gun, and Joe sat, feeling the water soak him up to his chest. While Vern held his gun on them, Chaplin tied Joe's outstretched hands to the piling in front of him.

"Your turn," Vern said to Frank.

As Chaplin tied Frank in the same way to the next piling, he said, "You'd better figure out how to hold your breath for six hours or so, because the tide is coming in and you'll be under water soon. We'll be back to pick up your bodies in the morning. And don't worry—we'll tell your parents you had a great time swimming before you drowned."

"Let's go." Auerbach walked away, followed by the other two. None of them looked back.

Already Joe felt the level of the water begin to climb higher. The bigger waves washed over his shoulders. Joe looked at his brother, wondering how long it would be before he could no longer see Frank's head.

Chapter

18

JOE TWISTED HIS HEAD around and saw the cars
drive away. He tried moving his arms, but the
rope was strong, and the knots were solid. He
flexed his hands to keep the circulation going.

"Frank? How are you doing?"

"Okay," he answered over the sound of the
waves. "Think there's any chance we can get to
our feet?"

"No way," Joe said. "The rope is too tight.
It won't slide up the piling."

Joe had a sudden flash of panic as the water
crept higher. There must be a way out of this,
he told himself. There's got to be.

He tried to rotate his body, hoping the friction
of the rope against the rough piling might weaken
it. Suddenly a stabbing pain shot through his
forearm. He gasped.

"What's the matter?" called Frank.

"I just got jabbed by something—like a splinter. Wait a second."

Joe twisted until his forearm came in contact with the sharp point again.

"I think it's some kind of staple, with one end sticking out of the piling. I'm going to try to get the sharp end into the knot and loosen it."

"I'm with you," called Frank.

Working carefully so as not to snap off the point, Joe struggled to move his arms until the knot was positioned over the piece of jagged metal. It was slow, frustrating work, and the water was continuing to rise.

"Frank! I think I've started it—"

"All right!" Frank exclaimed. A high wave broke over him and drenched his head.

The water had reached Joe's chin when he felt the knot loosen enough for him to work his hands free.

"I've got it!" he yelled. "One more minute—"

"A minute is all we've got," Frank sputtered, spitting out a mouthful of the Pacific.

Thirty seconds later Joe ripped himself free of the binding rope. "We're safe!" he whooped, leaping through the water to untie Frank. He got the rope undone just as Frank's mouth was completely submerged. With Joe's help Frank stood, gasping and choking.

"Let's get out of here," Frank croaked, stumbling toward shore. "Somehow I'm not in the mood for a swim."

Soaked, the Hardys staggered up the beach

toward the road. There they tried to flag down a passing car. The first few whizzed by. Then an old station wagon slowed and pulled over. Frank laughed as he recognized the surfers with their boards on the roof rack.

"You dudes again!" said the guy in the passenger's seat, hanging out the window. "What is it this time, you've been taking an evening dip?"

"It'd take too long to explain," Joe said through chattering teeth. "Can you drive us south a few miles?"

"Absolutely," the driver replied. "There are towels in the back."

Frank told the driver they were headed for the South Coast Surf Club, and he offered to drop them off right in front. As they neared the club, Frank leaned forward and said, "You can let us off just past the parking lot."

As they passed the lot, Joe and Frank peered out the window at the early evening.

"There's Auerbach's car and ours, over by Chaplin's trailer," Joe said.

The driver pulled off the road and the Hardys climbed out. "Take it easy, now," the driver's friend said. "And, hey, get out of those wet clothes."

"If you'd like to help a little more—"

"Let's have it, man," said the driver. "Our schedule is totally clear."

"Go to the nearest phone and call the Laguna Beach police. Tell Detective O'Boyle to meet

Frank and Joe at the Surf Club right away. And to bring friends. Got it?"

"Got it," said the driver. "Take it easy."

The old wagon took off.

"Let's go," Joe said to his brother.

The Hardys ran to the edge of the parking lot, and then jogged quietly toward Chaplin's trailer in the early gloom. As they neared it, they heard muffled voices—and Vern's sharp laugh.

Frank and Joe darted close to the trailer's metal wall, out of the occupants' line of sight if any of them looked out the window.

"Okay," Frank whispered. "Now we just hold on until—"

The trailer door opened. Vern Elliott came out, casually holding his shotgun with the barrel down. Frank, who was closer to the front steps, sprang up as Vern sensed a presence and spun around. Vern's eyes widened in shock.

"Hey! It's *them!*" he screamed. He tried to bring up the shotgun.

Frank leapt forward and hit Vern knee-high with his shoulder. The shotgun went off with a deafening roar as Frank's momentum carried him and Vern off the steps and onto the pavement. The gun hit the ground and Vern took a swing at Frank's head, which missed. He locked his legs around Frank's waist and began to squeeze.

Meanwhile, Joe had moved forward next to the door. When Ken Chaplin, pistol in hand, came into the doorway, Joe leapt up and hooked a hand into the filmmaker's belt. He yanked him forward and out of the trailer, sending him sprawling to the ground.

Chaplin got to his knees and lunged for his dropped gun, but Joe was on him and hauled him upright. A short left hook connected with Chaplin's stomach, and he gasped and crumpled to the ground. Joe scooped up the weapon.

"Aaaaugh!" Frank shouted as Vern tried to squeeze his hands around his throat. Frank brought his own hands up hard and broke the hold. He landed a hard left jab to Vern's nose, followed by a looping right that caught him on the point of the chin. Vern collapsed into a limp heap.

As Joe was finishing Chaplin off, he saw Auerbach take off and jump into his car. The car fishtailed with a squeal of tires as it headed for the parking lot entrance.

But before it got there, three police cruisers blocked the path, sirens wailing and lights flashing. O'Boyle and Ericsson leapt out of one of the cars as Auerbach screeched to a halt in front of them.

As Frank and Joe walked toward them, Auerbach got out of his car with a smile on his face.

"Officers!" said Auerbach. "I can explain everything. These two criminals, Chaplin and his henchman, have tried to incriminate me in their plot, and I want to file a complaint—"

"He lies," said Nadia Galinova, getting out of a police car and causing Auerbach to stop in midsentence with his mouth open. "He tells nothing but lies. It is *he* who is the worst criminal. He made others do his evil work, but now I will tell everything, and he will go to jail."

Auerbach spread his hands wide and tried to smile, but the smile was shaky.

"Hey, now, come on! Who are you going to believe, here? She's not even an American—"

"I will become one," Nadia countered regally. "Frank has convinced me. It's time to stop hiding and living in the past."

Frank answered her grateful smile with a very astonished one of his own as he realized she had gathered the courage to approach the police on her own. "That's great!" he blurted out, turning to see if Joe realized what had happened.

But now that he knew Auerbach had been captured, Joe had other things on his mind.

"Quick," he muttered to Frank. "Is there a working phone in Chaplin's trailer?"

"Yeah," Frank answered. "Why?"

"I've got to call Chris and tell her to heat up dinner."

Two hours later Auerbach, Chaplin, and Elliott had been carted off to jail, and the Hardys had told O'Boyle the whole story. "Two dozen times," Joe told Chris over a delicious, if slightly lukewarm, dinner at Tammy's house.

"But what about Nadia?" Chris asked urgently. "Are they going to arrest her?"

"No way," said Frank, swallowing a mouthful

of steak. "O'Boyle said he'd help her through the process of getting her sister naturalized if she cooperates in the Auerbach case."

"I still can't believe you guys are detectives!" Tammy said, leaning back in her chair and grinning at them. "You look so—well, kind of *goofy* to solve mysteries for a living."

"Gee, thanks, Tammy," Frank said. "If it makes you feel better, we don't do it for a living yet. We're still in school, remember."

"Chris doesn't think I'm goofy looking, do you, Chris?" Joe demanded, grinning goofily at Tammy's partner.

Chris smiled at him across the table. Frank could see that Joe was going to have a hard time saying goodbye to Chris.

"No, Joe, I don't think you're goofy," she said solemnly. "Look—you've saved the volleyball tournament and helped Tammy fight off a couple of kidnappers and taken me out for a great date. There's just one thing not so great about you, in fact—"

Everyone at the table waited tensely for Chris's final judgment.

"Well?" Joe demanded. "What is it?"

"You still can't catch a volleyball to save your life."

As Joe tossed a blizzard of crumpled paper napkins at Chris, the table erupted in laughter.

Frank and Joe's next case:

Frank and Joe take off on a cross-country ski-
ing trip into the Colorado Rockies and soon
find themselves facing the greatest challenge
of all: a test of survival! They've befriended
conservationist K. D. Becker, a woman dedi-
cated to saving the endangered mountain lion.
But K.D.'s been shot—and now it's *her* life
that hangs in the balance.

The boys discover that K.D.'s mission to cre-
ate a wildlife preserve has stirred up passions
as old as the frontier itself. Ranchers, hunters,
and native Americans all want the land—and
K.D. stands in the way. The hunt is on, and
the Hardys are hot on the trail of a suspect.
But the shooter's not about to give in without
a fight, and now Frank and Joe have become
fair game . . . in *Open Season,* Case #59 in
The Hardy Boys Casefiles™.